THE
AMERICAN
SATAN

THE AMERICAN SATAN

Kirby Farrell

WALKER & COMPANY
New York

Copyright © 1990 by Kirby Farrell

All rights reserved. No part of this book may be reproduced or transmitted in any form or by any means, electronic or mechanical, including photocopying, recording, or by any information storage and retrieval system, without permission in writing from the Publisher.

All the characters and events portrayed in this work are fictitious.

First published in the United States of America in 1990 by Walker Publishing Company, Inc.

Published simultaneously in Canada by Thomas Allen & Son Canada, Limited, Markham, Ontario

Library of Congress Cataloging-in-Publication Data

Farrell, Kirby, 1942–
The American Satan / Kirby Farrell.
ISBN 0-8027-5756-1
I. Title.
PS3556.A77A8   1990
813'.54—dc20   89-24994
CIP

Printed in the United States of America

2 4 6 8 10 9 7 5 3 1

For Susan

THE AMERICAN SATAN

Chapter One

From this wing of the hospital the construction site below was a mysterious bomb crater, as if one of the imitation Greek temples down there in the Harvard medical complex had blown up. No telling what would fill the hole. One more highrise presumably, like the ones flattened against Boston's harbor skyline in a spiky bar graph of strike-it-rich prosperity.

The lady beside me in the waiting room was warning me not to miss the rum-mangoes in the casino in Aruba if I ever got to the Caribbean. I gave my sacred promise. She recommended the broiled fish but not the spicy Mexican dishes that sat out on the table for hours. The flies, you know.

"Uh-oh," she groaned. "Look. It's raining."

"Just spitting." I shrugged. "Spring shower."

"It's radioactive. The TV says so."

"Ever since Chernobyl," I said, "I've stopped drinking out of puddles."

My fellow survivor gave a grim little sniff: "Look at the atom-bomb plants out in Colorado. And Carolina. Billions they want to clean the contamination. If it can ever be cleaned up. And look at the leaks down at Pilgrim—

how far's Plymouth, thirty miles? Do you know what the leukemia rate is around that plant? And the taxpayers—do you hear any screaming?"

"There's a lot of confusion out there," I said.

The woman cleared her throat: "If nobody does anything, you won't be able to go outside. You'll get cancer."

Her eyes shimmered. Not contact lenses—she wore glasses with pink-tinted polygonal lenses—but tears. Was she a visitor like me, or a paying customer? Her expensive silver hair and blue suit introduced her as a businesswoman. Her lapel sported a gold pin in the shape of a pyramid with a staring eyeball in the peak: familiar symbol to every lover of the dollar bill. Even her makeup meant business, the eyebrows and mouth drawn a little too bold, as if to show time who was still boss. In her embarrassment she shifted her worries to the doorway:

"Ah. Poor dear."

As I looked up two orderlies wheeled a dolly past. The poor dear was an assortment of bandages and casts with my ex-wife's dark brown hair sticking out one end. Some things you can never really prepare for. I had the desperate feeling you get when a dump truck backs over your heart. I made it to the door before they shooed me back inside to wait. "This place is murder," the woman said. "Let's hope she has insurance."

"I'll have to find out," I said.

"You're an investigator."

"As a matter of fact. I'm also her husband."

"Oh, I'm sorry."

"Ex-husband actually."

"I am sorry." She sounded as if divorce was worse than any bodily smash-up. But she recovered fast: "What do you investigate?"

"Nowadays mostly business fraud. Usually out of New York. I'm in Boston because a drunk driver put Meg off the road last night. And you?"

Dorothy O'Hare, her name was. "My daughter likes to keep me waiting." She smiled. "She's a doctor."

"Maybe we're waiting for the same doc."

Dorothy O'Hare dug a breath mint out of her purse. And a photo. "That's Carol."

A coed in a cap and gown. Glamorous pose from the Studio of Fabian Bachrach: mug shots of debutantes and gods. But the girl in the photo didn't need any darkroom diddling: she had peach-blossom skin and a mouth that made your lips tingle. With her neck arched, she seemed to be glancing backward, thrilled to discover you there. I confessed: "She's beautiful."

The proud mother sucked on the breath mint: "Good looks are a curse."

"Millionaires say that about money."

"It's true. Any moron will chase a pretty face. Like Jerry, the one she married. Even now she's scarcely got rid of him. You wouldn't think doctors would be such babies, would you?"

You never know. One of my first clients, the retired Dr. Milton Posnik, beat his wife senseless with his cane one Sunday night in Wellesley, then regretted it with a bottle of Darvons. This relieved his suspicion that his wife was trying to poison his food. For weeks the two of them had been partying in bed with the help of his prescription pad and Scotland's finest distilleries, the bed sheets pinch-hitting for the bathroom tissues and the kitchen wall-to-wall with garbage bags inspected by the Saint Bernard who, like his master, hadn't been outdoors in months.

A couple of doctors appeared in the waiting-room

doorway. One was the tall and reddish-blond Carol. Dorothy O'Hare began fishing in her handbag: "You say you're an investigator."

I nodded: "But I don't usually do son-in-laws."

She placed another breath mint on her tongue, fastidiously, the way you'd put a mouse dropping in an ashtray. "But you're, well, legitimate. Licensed or whatever."

I gave her one of my cards: "The working agreement comes with references. We specialize in credit-card fraud, light-fingered cashiers, warehouse hijackers. You name it."

"Duncan Ames," she read to herself. "Security Analysts." She took a gold-plated mechanical pencil out of her handbag.

"The pyramid on your pen," I said, "it matches the one on your pin."

"It's an organization. For bookkeepers." She held my card with her thumb, on end, like a playing card. "I could use help," she said. "I—we—it's a matter of threats."

"Who's threatening who?"

"I suppose you must charge a fortune. Is it by the hour or—?"

"Mrs. O'Hare, let's stop tap dancing. What's on your mind?"

"If I paid you two hundred to start, could you help me?"

"Help you what?"

"There could be a lot of money in it for you. I can tell you that much right now. There's huge sums at stake."

In my mind's eye I pictured pirates dragging a heavy chest ashore at Revere Beach.

"If I only knew who to trust," she demanded opening her wallet. She thumbed out ten twenties. "Here's how serious I am."

Armed with her clipboard, Dr. Carol strolled into the waiting room. With the fancy gold pencil her mother jotted an address on the back of my card and tore it off for me. "Here. I live in Newton Center. Can you come by today? Do you have time?"

What I had was a daughter looking at college catalogs and an ex-wife who would be wearing plaster for months. And while I was visiting Boston, no clients. So I said, "I'll stop by after supper."

"It's the threats. I can't stand the threats." Anger crackled in the back of her throat now. To her daughter she called musically, "You're late. As usual. Just as well. I've been having a very nice conversation."

Chapter Two

According to her name tag, Carol was Dr. C. Schell—either not yet divorced or keeping her married name for simplicity's sake. She walked her mother out into the corridor, hand around her shoulder, a sympathetic send-off for a cranky patient. I gave them a head start.

When I caught up, Dr. C was alone at the nurses' station.

"You're Dr. Seashell?"

Her eyes startled. When I indicated her name tag she had the grace to grin with me. We sat on stools at the counter, not quite face-to-face. Up this close she wasn't quite the studio princess in her mother's photo. You could see night shifts under her eyes and the long winter in her complexion; her nose wasn't so perfect. On the other hand, her hair had a reddish glint more distinctive than the tinsel in the portrait, and you couldn't miss the intelligence in her eyes. As I'd guessed, she had Meg on her clipboard.

"So you're the husband?"

"Once upon a time."

"You're lucky to be alive."

"Meg's a real man-eater all right."

She was flustered: "You weren't in the accident with her?"

"I just drove in from New York. To help put the pieces back together."

"Ah, too bad."

"Too bad I wasn't in the accident?"

"We could have put you both in one cast," she said tartly. "A big saving."

"We've already spent too much time in the same cast. We're divorced."

"We shouldn't be kidding around. At least not until Mrs. Ames is out of danger." Suddenly she was all doctor again. The twinkle in her eye grew fixed as if she were peering through a scope at my naked retina. It was my turn to stammer:

"I thought the Emergency Room doctors—"

"Don't quote me, but down there if you're not dead you're in great shape." She was watching my face. "I didn't mean to alarm you. It's just that she's more than a little banged up."

The conversation skidded into medical terms: hemorrhage and contusion and fracture.... The windshield had put up quite a fight, knocking out a couple teeth and—my heart stumbled—Meg's left eye. The steering wheel had gone for the heart and other plumbing.

In her grim objectivity Dr. Schell was subtly scolding the world and the flesh for its weaknesses. Typical doctor. At the same time she touched my wrist lightly: "I'm sorry, I didn't mean to shock you. We'll do our damndest not to lose her. But she won't be out of bed soon. Maybe not till summer. You should know."

"My daughter will be rattled."

"Tell her to come see me. I'll reassure her."

It was a personal moment, nose-to-nose. Then the kettle began shrieking on a hot plate behind the counter. Dr. C flopped tea bags into two paper cups. I said, "Looks like I stick around Boston awhile."

"What sort of work do you do?"

"I'm an investigator."

"Of what?"

"Business mysteries usually."

"Was that your card my mother had?"

"You have sharp eyes."

Worry flicked across Carol's face: "She tell you what's wrong?"

"You don't have any idea?"

"New doctors get worked around the clock. I feel guilty I get so out of touch."

I took a chance: "Your mother says she's being threatened."

"God, not by little green men, I hope. I see so many old people in here with delusional symptoms." Dr. C gave me a look of comic alarm: "But I hope it's not a real threat either."

"She thinks the rain out there will give her cancer."

"Maybe she's right. How much of the official news do you believe?"

"I told her I'd stop by later today."

"If it's, you know, if it turns out to be important, please tell me. Okay?"

I nodded and changed the subject: "You play tennis."

We looked at her tennis shoes together, then she grinned: "Where I live, our building has a rooftop court. You can see the whole harbor. You feel on top of the world when you get a piece of the ball. Do you play?"

"I work too hard."

"So do I. The doctor of the future will be a computer you consult over the phone. It's already happening."

"And I have a bum shoulder. Old gator-wrestling injury."

"Look at me."

"My pleasure."

She gave me a complicated stare. "You really do need to straighten up. Shall I prescribe some exercises?" As she got up she straightened my shoulders, her fingers pressing behind my neck. "That's better." Then she gave my stomach a friendly poke and grinned: "I've been on duty for about twenty hours running, so you could straighten up my posture too."

"Any time."

She took a healthy breath that made the chest pockets of her white coat stand out in a very female way: "Your wife's in Room 557."

Chapter Three

"Shouldna come," Meg said. Her jaw was fractured. One brown eye stared out of the bandages: "Good you to come."

I shrugged: "You'll be back to work in no time. Enjoy the vacation."

"Rachel all right?"

"Very brave. I thought I'd stick around to help you guys."

"No need."

She tried to shake her head. Nothing if not self-reliant is Margaret Nilsson Ames. Her father built houses all over the north shore and retired to Florida, keeping up his feud with Meg. He'd always resented her marriage, but he didn't approve of the divorce either. Once every year or two they got together long-distance to tell each other off. Meg tried to cough:

"What time sit? Afnoon?"

I knew her too well. Looking at her I was sore all over, as if her body was silently communicating with mine. Flesh of my flesh. One flesh, one pain. As the protective stupidity of shock began to wear off I could see it wasn't just physical pain waiting for me either. Maybe if you're divorced long enough—a hundred years, say—you finally get more objective.

"Hoor Rachel."

"She'll be all right."

"Haven't hin hery good nother. No tine to talk her."

"We can tell what's on your mind."

"At's ut you think." She added: "I lived if you."

"You must be thirsty. Want a sip of water?"

"Sishteen years."

"I'll get a straw from the nurse."

"You still nad at ne?"

I shook my head. Looking back, it had been a quiet war, an almost friendly divorce. Only after the crisis was past did either of us admit the ache. I put my hand in the crook of her arm above the IV needle, where the pulse flicked. Her eye glistened. She said: "A drunk hit ne."

"A priest."

"A—?"

"From Framingham. He'd been out with friends playing cards and getting fall-down drunk last night."

"He all right?"

"Bruises and banged-up conscience."

"Hoor guy."

"The archdiocese will probably settle out of court."

They were wheeling supper trays around in the hall when Rachel came in. Usually she has her mother's thick dark red hair and good looks. Today her hair shot up in greenish punk whorls as if an iguana were basking on her noggin. Her spangled dress was perfect for a palm reader in an Alabama trailer park. Rachel had her mother's bluntness too. Three steps into the room she stopped short:

"God, you look awful!"

Rather than kiss bandages, Rachel put her cheek on

Meg's hand. Then she fingered the plastic IV tube and touched the bandaged jaw. "I'll diet too," she said. "We can both diet."

She said hello to me. She hadn't really hugged me since the divorce.

Chapter Four

Step out of Brigham and Women's Hospital at dusk, the streetcar clacking between the red-brick storefronts on Huntington Avenue, and you could be walking into your own childhood again, when Coke was a dime but you guzzled Moxie or Orange Crush. In my high-school days the hospital was still Peter Bent Brigham, and when we passed it sneaking in town to the burlesque show one of the wiseguys in the car would quip: 'Peter Bent Brigham and Brigham loved it.' Now the sky was clearing and darkening. As Rachel and I headed into the suburbs on Route 9, I remembered Dorothy O'Hare. "I have to make a business call in Newton."

"Work work work," Rachel grumbled. It was an old grudge.

"Afterward I'll treat us to a Szechuan feed at the Golden Dragon. Although it's risky. Your green hairdo may end up stir-fried with bamboo shoots."

"What's wrong with my hair?" She was daring me.

"It's dangerous to go around impersonating an asparagus."

"How about a grown-up man pretending he's a dumb

bloodhound sniffing the butts of crooked capitalists. Now that's weird."

"It's got to be done."

"Oh sure. The bloodhound barks at a bunch of little crooks so poor people will keep believing in the system and the real crooks can do what they want."

"Which is?"

"Like killing. Like in Guatamala them killing that Quaker guy who was helping the peasants build windmills."

"I missed that one."

"Sure. Because who owns the newspapers. You know what they did, don't you? They kidnapped this guy and taped his hands behind his back and forced a stick of dynamite into his mouth, and—"

Beside me in the gloom her hands traced a silent, hideous explosion. As she got older I was less sure which of us was the naive one. All my retorts seemed lame. Finally I said, "I thought your generation was supposed to be me-first conservatives."

She shrugged: "Everybody's not the same."

"Doing any sketching these days?"

She grunted: "I packed all that garbage away."

"How come?"

"It kept coming out, like, deformed. Besides, it's just an escape, it's not real."

"Put the real stuff on the page."

She sighed tolerantly: "People don't want to see it. They think you're pretentious."

"It'll be different when you get to college."

"Oh sure. The kids I know, the ones applying, they all want to be management and marketing majors. So they can write memos and sell shit all their lives. Barf."

"Times changed to get this way. They'll change again."
"Oh forget it," she huffed.

In Newton Corner I looked for Cedar Street—one of those tree names that usually means an older neighborhood. But in the end I had to call the cops from a pay phone to get directions.

The O'Hare house was a dignified Victorian affair with a front porch—"piazza," we used to say—as wide as a hooped skirt. Rachel cranked her seat down and the radio up to wait.

The lights were on. Dorothy had left the door ajar for me. The only doorbell was a shiny brass replica of the original gizmo: a thumbscrew that gave a low ratchety burp when you twisted it. In the foyer was a gloomy Victorian hall stand and an inside door with oval glass. I gave the doorknob a twist and yodeled. The hall smelled of burned supper.

The living room featured tastefully fake antiques. A fancy cabinet disguised the television. The tufted chairs were perfect for ruling an empire. In a gilt frame on the coffee table sat a blowup of Carol's graduation pose and a gilt ceramic vase with real flowers. There were little porcelain figures displayed on the wainscotting that ran around the room: girls and boys and other quaint animals.

I found the owner of this tidy dollhouse around the corner at the dining-room table, all by herself. She had fallen into her plate of soup. At least her head lay in the plate, nose down, like a fantastic dumpling. The right lens of her glasses was submerged in soup. One hand rested politely in her lap, the other curled around the glass saltshaker. Brownish onion soup spattered the tablecloth, and a darker stain was still seeping into her lap. Her eyes were open. She was getting cold. Touch her and she would spill onto the floor. Except for the neat puncture at the base of her skull and the messy exit wound, she looked ludicrous: granny in her cups.

It crossed my mind that other guests might still be on the premises. I felt the special indigestion that comes with the thought of a swan dive into a plate of onion soup, and regretted my prejudice against the workaday handgun.

In the kitchen I found a Lean Cuisine frozen dinner beginning to smoke in the oven. The Florentine Chicken label on the carton would have tasted better than the parched pulp in the aluminum tray. The oven had been on a good hour. Her handbag leaned against a bruised golden delicious apple on the counter, breath mints and wallet still in it.

I used the wall phone to dial 911. While I was waiting for the cops I tried to call Carol, but the switchboard at the hospital was defensive about private phone numbers, so I had to let them beep her. Don't call us, we'll call you.

Upstairs I found Carol's bedroom more or less as she must have left it to go to college. There were porcelain birds on the dresser, a crocheted snowflake hanging from a lampshade, a couple of pretty cacti on the windowsill, and in one bookshelf, between a biology text and a fat *Gone with the Wind,* a plastic human skeleton the size of an iguana's. No dolls. On the nightstand sat a stuffed bear with a handkerchief knotted around his nose to fix a head cold.

Leaning in the car window, I said to Rachel, "This is going slower than I expected. The woman's dead."

"Oh yuck! Heart attack?"

"Bullet in the neck."

"God. Like an execution."

"Exactly."

"This a drug thing?"

"Doubtful."

"How long's it going to take?"

A child of the TV age, I thought, expecting a sixty-minute answer for every horror. With time out for ads.

The Newton cops fielded an enthusiastic team. They directed me to study the Big Dipper from Dorothy's veranda while they took turns with a flashlight examining the door for signs of forced entry. I overheard the detective in charge worrying about a gang of Cuban boatlift refugees who worked out of Boston, specialized in housebreaks and, having nothing left to lose, killed anything that spooked them.

The state cops sent a Lieutenant Phil Auburn, who sported tightly clipped gray hair and smoke-puff eyebrows. He was getting over a cold so his baritone commands scraped like a shovel on a cement walk. He shot Dorothy with a Polaroid camera and wrote her up in his notebook, while two rookies cruised from room to room amazed that nothing had been ransacked.

With all of us the lieutenant tried for automatic dominance. Somehow I knew better than to offer a handshake—just as well, since he preferred to stare at my ID and make me repeat my story to test my IQ.

After I described my conversation at the hospital Lieutenant Auburn shook his head: "If the victim was already feeling threatened, this is no routine break-in."

I didn't disagree.

Rachel appeared in the doorway to the front hall. She stood there, cagey and curious and awed by death. When the phone rang in the hall the lieutenant took it. He hung up announcing, "That's the victim's daughter. She's a doctor. She'll be here soon as she gets someone to cover for her."

Easier said than done apparently. I'd just come back from driving Rachel home to Natick when Carol finally showed up.

Chapter Five

She handled the shock by being the good doctor. Though the dining room was off-limits, she headed straight for it. She even examined the gunshot wound for a moment as if to satisfy herself that it really was true.

Lieutenant Auburn said, "Wait. You can't touch her."

"Ah," she gasped. "The medical examiner has to—"

"Right. It won't be long."

Carol stared into her mother's face with clinical care and eyes shiny with pain. The local cops watched her with uncomfortable respect.

It was like an inquest, the new doctor and the state cop each puzzling out loud. Dorothy O'Hare had been twenty years a widow. For years she'd been the bookkeeper for a Brookline chiropractor. She was a serious bridge player, with tournament rank. Maybe half a dozen times a year she and an old girlfriend or two signed up for gambling jaunts to Atlantic City, Las Vegas, and Aruba. The lieutenant's eyebrows hopped. Carol headed him off.

"My mother had a good head for numbers. She loved games. But she wasn't a compulsive."

"No IOUs or like that?"

"Of course not." Her eyes filled.

The medical examiner came and examined and signed. Like a scorekeeper, he made the murder official. The lumpish form sprawled on the table became history. The emergency wagon arrived and went. The questions grew mundane: who signs what, how do you manage a funeral.

Carol and I were left to lock up. The porch was black and creaky. There was a smudge of cloud on the moon. I said, "The cops admire the way you kept your head."

"I wanted to let go like a baby."

"The cops act cool but they feel the pain too."

"I kept pretending it was the hospital and I didn't really know this patient." The deadbolt made a scratchy clack in the door. She sucked in a deep breath: "I was afraid if I let go, I wouldn't stop. I'd just go to pieces."

"You can't always be on duty."

"A doctor can't afford to get carried away."

"It's the same in my business."

"But you give the impression you're all there."

"Your mother must have thought so when she hired me this afternoon."

"Mother never said why she wanted to see you tonight?"

"I wish I knew."

We stood on the porch, under the spotted moon, paralyzed in different ways. At last Carol said, "Well, you want to get going."

I didn't move.

"I can't afford to pay an investigator, Mr. Ames. I'll have to trust the police to handle this."

"Your mother and I have a contract. She paid me enough to ask a few questions."

"God, it seems weird to think of paying money to understand someone's death. But I suppose that's what medicine's about, too."

"What kind of an accountant was your mother?"

"She never worked for any gangsters, if that's what you're getting at. She had a habit of trying to beat the IRS for a few bucks every April, so she got audited regularly. But that's the extent of her crimes."

"Friends?"

"She was active in good causes. United Fund. Catholic Relief. League of Women Voters."

"What's her boss like, the chiropractor?"

"Dr. Farhat? She thinks the world of him." Carol sucked in a breath: "Thought the world. I just hope—" She hesitated. "Look."

There were curious neighbors out on the sidewalk under the streetlight. I said, "Let's have a drink."

"Now? Maybe I could use some tea."

"My car's in the driveway. Follow me."

We made it as far as Newton Corner looking for a late-night spot, when all at once Dr. C's BMW tooted and peeled off toward Boston. My old Volvo grunted along behind, my foot on the floor.

In town the Prudential tower hovered over Back Bay, lights on, windows glimmering like gold coins spilled out of a rip in the heavens.

The BMW's taillights stopped before a new apartment highrise beyond Mystic Wharf in the harbor. Elite turf: a yuppy tenement. A kind of credit card raised a steel portcullis, letting her into an underground garage. I parked in the street.

Dr. C was locking her doc bag in the BMW's trunk when I rattled the steel cage and called her name. She came over looking exhausted and faintly irritable, but game. "You really want that drink, don't you?"

"Were you taking the lead back there or waving sayonnara?"

"I wanted to get home before I fell asleep at the wheel."

"I'll take off then. I misunderstood." I fished out my car keys again: "What did you start to say back there? You just hoped something or other."

"Did I?"

"How does your husband get along with your mother?"

"Jerry and I go to divorce court next month. It's no big trauma. Mostly just hard bargaining."

I nodded: "Your mother despised him."

"She told you that?" Her mouth took a rueful tuck in one corner: "My mother used to commiserate with Jerry about my failings. And with me about his. Mothers sometimes play for sympathy. It's no fun to get old." She motioned me toward the elevator. "You might as well come on up for a minute."

She poked her plastic card into the control box, a motor hummed, and the portcullis rose. At the elevator she thumped the Up button. The machinery grunted and stalled. "This dump," she growled. "You pay a fortune for a maintenance-free place, and you get a ninety-ninth-floor walk-up."

"Then why stay?"

"It's safe. If you're a woman physician in a big hospital, you appreciate a little extra security. Especially tonight." Again she smacked the button with her palm. "The only thing is, if this automatic lifestyle breaks down, boy are you helpless."

The elevator door slid open. I said, "So your mother never really liked your husband."

"Oh they got along. Dorothy wasn't a very brave meanie. She was more the sneaky-put-down type. She had a lot of frustrations, all her life."

Carol's apartment was feminine and pleasantly messy, with the odd magazine and unmated shoe holding out for real life. A maroon robe drooped from the sofa where she'd tossed it going off to work. The Oriental rug was a garden of flowers as intricately patterned as a computer circuit board. On the living-room wall were Persian miniatures that snagged your eye, and an African mask with spectacular teeth. "Dr. Farhat—my mother's boss—he's from Iran," Carol said prying off one shoe with the toe of the other. "He gave us tips about buying Persian things."

Tossing her hospital coat over the back of the chrome and leather armchair, she pulled on the robe from the sofa. She stepped lightly on the carpet. Its reds looked hot as campfire coals. On the balcony sat a cheap hibachi. At this height you felt airborne, as if you were bound for one of the exotic places in the travel books on the wall shelf. "I collect guides," she said. "To get to be a doctor, you have to postpone everything. But one of these days I'm going to do some real living."

When she drew the drapery cords, winged lions stretched out against golden heavens, floor to ceiling.

While Carol phoned the hospital to leave a message for her chief, I tried out the bathroom. Uninformative medicine chest. Diaphragm in a designer case of marbled plastic suitable for pearls. Generic aspirin, all-natural toothpaste, OTC pills for premenstrual cramps. Disposable razors for legs. In the bathtub, incongruous coal-tar dandruff shampoo plus the usual dainty hair suds.

"One glass," she said over the coffee table. "Then I have to sleep." She poured white wine: "It's tasty, nothing fancy. Comes from the Kaiserstuhl in Germany, from a farmer in Buchheim who makes his own. No additives. We brought back a few cases."

"We?"

"A friend and I. Not worth the customs hassle, as it turned out." Through the coffee table's glass top you could see her toes snuggled into the silky wool carpet. She watched me try the wine. "I'm doing cinnamon tea," she said. "Caffeine makes me shiver. And wine will give me a headache." She blinked as if to be sure I was really there. "It's so late maybe I'll just have a cup of hot water with some lemon. It warms you up."

I must have smiled, because suddenly she was self-conscious.

"Hot water. That really does sound asinine. Gimme the wine, Joe." She reached across the table for the bottle with a wise-guy glint in her eye. "So what are you doing here? Really."

"Thinking about murder. And you."

"Thinking about murdering me?"

"Wondering who might want to hurt you. Your husband, say?"

"Jerry's a lawyer." She didn't exactly sneer.

"What kind of law?"

"He's with Dewey, Screwam, and Howe."

"Otherwise known as?"

"Barnet, Moser, and Schell."

"He's a partner?"

She nodded. "He's doing all right now. Finally."

"Your mother blamed him for a lot of—"

"My mother had heavy-duty opinions. Not a monster or anything, but opinionated. Hyde Park Irish. Jerry's like me, very independent. Which is probably why he attracted me. And why we drove each other nuts."

"Does he lose his temper?"

"Jerry? Not the way you mean."

"Ever hear him argue with your mother?"

In her glass the wine had a rosy hue. She took a sip and changed the subject: "I had the impression someone was in the house when my mother got home."

"Possibly."

"And crept up behind her."

I nodded: "It was a kind of execution."

"Jesus." Carol's voice suffocated in her throat. "I'm having a bad reaction to this."

"Sorry." I put my hand on her forearm. "I'm just wondering who could approach her in such a—"

"Okay, okay," she protested. She clamped her hands under her arms. Her mouth twisted. "None of this is real to me yet. I haven't even begun to . . . I owe her . . . everything happens so fast. I feel so selfish. All we ever did was get ready to live. We dreamed what it would be like once we . . . But this—"

A little wave of her hand swept the rug, the room, the whole yuppie paradise into Boston Harbor. Her voice sputtered out. Figure Carol was grieving not only for her mother but also for the years they'd spent pushing for her success: for the little girl with the plastic skeleton on her dresser and the dopey bear with the schnozz rag. Sometimes the thought of death is a fall down a psychic elevator shaft. Even if you're in the business. I found myself almost whispering, "Carol, if I can help, here's a number, phone me."

"It's hard for doctors . . . you know, asking."

"You're too smart to want a lot of babbled consolations. But, well, beyond that."

I might have hugged her, but the woman—nobody's daughter anymore—bolted into the kitchen to pour the tea and keep her tears to herself.

Chapter Six

After driving Rachel to school in the morning, I unpacked my computer to run a spreadsheet program designed to spot certain kinds of expense-account fudge. My partner Vera had written the program, and she insisted I sample it. Frankly I'd rather eat a vampire bat than do statistics, but Vera is determined to professionalize me.

I had trouble concentrating on the data. It might be a month, I thought restlessly, before I could leave Rachel and Meg and get back to work. And I thought about Dorothy O'Hare put to death in her own house, Mafia-style. Rarely do you become a target for no good reason. You can have the bad luck to meet an armed crazy who has just received his marching orders from God. Drunken headlights can hump you on their way home from happy hour. But people don't die randomly in a plate of soup.

After school I dropped Rachel at Longwood so she could take the trolley into Brigham and Women's, then I crossed Brookline to pay a call on Dr. Mehdi Farhat, ace chiropractor and bereaved employer.

He had bought the old Olaf Thorsson estate in Brookline, including old Olaf's collection of antique fire engines and five pricey acres of backyard by Watteau. The street corner displayed a tasteful Crimewatch sign, and the circular driveway a pint-size white Chem-Lawn tank truck. The house combined the best features of Boston Garden and the Parthenon, but Dr. Farhat and his associates adjusted patients across the lawn in a white clapboard building that could have been a Puritan meeting house.

The waiting room had a businesslike posture chart on the wall, and a rack of New Age health magazines mixed with issues of *People* and *Money*. A waiting patient was leafing through a house brochure whose cover showed Mehdi lecturing to a medical convention on a rooftop patio with the Eiffel Tower over his shoulder. Glossy pics caught Mehdi in guest spots captioned by his first name: "Mehdi on Channel 7's *Medical Beat*"; "Mehdi at Holy Rosary Society Luncheon." News clippings listed the charities and civic organizations he'd succored. On the back page he was accepting a scroll in a Statehouse ceremony, both arms flung skyward like a presidential nominee or Mighty Mouse.

Even in the flesh the man was radiant. He seemed bigger than he was because he pumped your hand passionately, as if pulling you out of a collapsed coal mine. A man around my age, maybe forty. Greek-looking or Italian, with a long movie-star nose and a soothing, slightly accented voice colored by British vowels.

"The daughter called me, the doctor, Carol. I can't believe it, it's so stupid, like something in Beruit, a car bomb or something. Crazy fanatics. I was just in Beruit." He emphasized his amazement by touching his fingertips to his bristly black hair: "Mrs. O'Hare was very close to my heart, like someone in my own family. She had Thanksgiving dinner in my house. Where do I find the person who can replace her? She ran all my office business."

"Business looks good."

"When you can relieve pain, people are grateful. I have five practitioners working with me here. We need more room."

His smile was a heat lamp relaxing me. He wanted to know all about the business of business investigations. I pressed him fairly hard, but he knew nothing about any threats, nothing about a resentful son-in-law. Nor did he know who I was working for, which made him nervous. He did ascertain that I have a slight scoliosis and should sit straight.

"You'll be okay. Just don't slouch like heavy thoughts are weighing down your shoulders." He gave one overworked shoulder an amiable squeeze. "It's healthy to enjoy life. You know what I'm saying?"

He had the beginnings of a successful potbelly. I thanked him for the tips.

The son-in-law, Jerry Schell, had a secretary to bark at nuisance visitors. At Barnet, Moser, and Schell the setup was essentially a warren of back rooms festooned with New England totems: an antique cranberry scoop, prints of a McKay clipper ship and breakers at Ogunquit, and a hip-roofed Vermont barn in red acrylics. Everything but a glass-topped lobster trap for a coffee table.

Carol O'Hare had married a good-looking guy in his mid-thirties, though his face seemed held together by a sharp, narrow nose. He was in his big-city-lawyer uniform, tastefully pin-striped, sitting with his back to a tinted executive view of Marlboro Street. One hand cupped his handsome chin, the other hand propped up his elbow—as if he were talking to me on the telephone. On his desk, on a green blotter, sat a *Wall Street Journal* and a silver tray with a bottle of Perrier water on it.

No, the cops hadn't contacted him, though Carol had. To be blunt about it, he wasn't very fond of his mother-in-law. But he was sorry to hear the bad news: "Nobody's safe with all these animals out there ready to shark you for drug money. Look at Carol. Every day they jump doctors looking to grab drugs. I wouldn't have MD tags on my car if you paid me. That's like wearing a bull's-eye over your heart."

"What did Dorothy like to quarrel with you about?"

"We just had discussions. All the time, discussions. She was a bigot, you know. Snotty Irish Catholic. She had it in for blacks and PRs and Jews and you name it."

"How about her boss?"

"Who, the Iranian? She felt sorry for him. She started working for him when the Ayatollah was holding all those American hostages, and it was so bad for business that Farhat was thinking about having his name changed. She mothered him."

"So she wasn't a total bigot."

"What the hell, Farhat wasn't stealing her pride and joy."

"She didn't want you marrying her daughter."

He snorted. "How does she think *my* mother felt? Besides, she loved me once I was bringing home the bucks."

"Could Dorothy have written a gambling IOU she couldn't cover? On impulse maybe?"

"What's gambling? A Megabucks ticket? A few days in Atlantic City with an old girlfriend? Anyway, she had the money."

"Where'd she get it?"

That turned out to be the first of many things he didn't know. When I asked where he'd been the evening before, it was on the tip of his tongue: "Home. My apartment. Working on cases."

"Anyone see you at home?"

He bristled: "Look. You ask anybody here how busy I've been. Ask them if I've been chained to my desk for the last couple weeks. Twenty-four hours a day."

"You phone anyone last night who can—?"

"All kinds of people."

"You live in the suburbs?"

His hands came to life: "What is this crap! The address is in the phone book. Look it up. I've got work to do."

So I went over to the hospital to see Meg, and if possible Carol, feeling like Dorothy O'Hare wasn't going to get much justice for her two hundred bucks.

Chapter Seven

That's why the phone call surprised me. As I was burping the computer the next morning Dr. Mehdi Farhat called to request the pleasure of my company.

Just before noon he pulled me into his front hall with an enthusiastic handshake. Behind him a staircase swept up toward heaven. A rug on the wall sported a tree of paradise throbbing with color like a map of the arteries serving a thriving heart.

"Everybody calls me Mehdi," he insisted.

I joined the crowd.

Oriental carpets laid over one another absorbed our footsteps. In the shadowy living room silver and crystal glimmered. "Try this chair." He steered me. "It's healthy for your back. Designed by a world expert on the spine, Dr. Holacek, in Prague. But made in Sweden of course. Feel the leather. See, it pushes you here."

He gave me an educational shove in the small of the back.

"Have some lunch. You like lamb? How about with peppers and onion and tomato . . ." He was still listing ingredients as he disappeared into the kitchen to call for a guest plate. He came back with two tall rose-tinted glasses of fruit juice on a tray. A mixture of papaya and lime and stuff from the Garden of Eden. Mehdi made an informal toast with his glass: "When I need advice, I call on experts."

This cold-blooded flattery warmed my heart.

"Don't laugh," he said. "This is for me a nervous situation. I look like a rich man because I work hard, like all Americans. And because my name sounds like an Iranian, after that stupidity with the hostages and everything, people blamed me. It took three years to bring my practice back to life. And now again it starts."

Who didn't remember the TV mobs shouting, "Death to the American Satan"? After months of burning Uncle Sam dolls and swooning over their own revolutionary purity, the Ayatollah's faithful had bumped the American president from the White House. My next-door neighbor was upset enough to flaunt a bumper sticker on which Mickey Mouse was giving the Ayatollah the finger. Iran still held America's TV sets hostage; the current president had been caught begging Iran for favors and solemnly lied about it on the evening news.

"This is very bad," Mehdi groaned. "The president tries to bargain with Iran and still they keep the hostages in Lebanon. They make a fool of him. And people take out their stress on anyone connected with Iran, and that is me."

Something snapped in Mehdi's hallway, a loud electronic zap. I looked over to see a girl flash past the doorway firing a pistol at her reflection in the enormous gilt-edged mirror on the wall.

"Sari," Mehdi called. "Stop shooting yourself. Come meet Mr. Ames."

She was a skinny soda straw of a child, about seven,

with gold doodads in her hair. Close up her features were startlingly irregular, the nose and mouth crushed to one side as if an invisible hand were muzzling her face. She pressed her cheek against her father's pant leg and eyed me coolly: "Put a target on and I'll shoot you."

The pistol was a mock Beretta that fired a beam of infrared light. Hit the strap-on target and a sharp crack registered the kill. "These guns." Mehdi shuddered. "My son begged me for them. With his friends it's a fad. He goes to Groton. It's only pretend, he says, like TV, and he knows what's real and what's not. But I don't like them."

Sari's eyes flashed: "I bet I can kill you first."

"That's enough," Mehdi scolded. His hand searched downward until her jaw slipped into his palm. "Sari's mother lives in Los Angeles. A very social lady. I don't want my kids raised up by servants."

"I have a daughter," I offered. Sari wriggled free.

"Can she shoot?"

A hefty woman in a stylish housecoat brought in a tray of skewered lamb and coffee. Without any discussion she took Sari back to the kitchen with her.

"And now," Mehdi resumed, "now it's the crazy terrorists. And more hostages. Madmen blowing up airliners. Threatening innocent people. Totally insane."

From the pocket of his sport shirt he unfolded a sheet of lined schoolpaper. The message was spelled out in headline caps pasted in place:

DEATH TO YOU GO
HOME

It signed off in piecemeal type:

THE American satAN

"Messy paste job," I said. "Why that name?"

Mehdi shrugged: "That's what the Ayatollah Khomeini calls this country, the American Satan. Some crazy person must be offended. He wants revenge against Iran. He wants to kill me and my family like he killed Mrs. O'Hare."

"This isn't the first message," I guessed.

"There was one before. I thought it was just craziness, like filthy words in a public toilet. From this same Satan."

"Did you save that note?"

He fished in his pocket. Same lined white paper, same messy paste job:

>   GO home Arab sCUm
>   NO POLICE or You die

He was indignant: "I'm no Arab. Persians are not Arabs. We come from the Indo-European blood family. Here's the envelope."

It was a white cheapie, no watermark, canceled in Boston. I said, "Why didn't you tell me about this before?"

"Read the words. If I go to the police, they kill me. How can I be sure you will be careful enough not to do more harm?"

"But you're telling me now."

"Yes, since yesterday I've been thinking."

"Got any dissatisfied customers?"

"No, no. Not usually. Chiropractic isn't chemical like drug medicine. We treat the whole person. When I remove nerve blockages in the spine, I harmonize the mind too."

"Somebody out there still has a kink or two. Anyone ever threaten to sue you?"

"No, no. Oh, maybe one or two impatient people, they want miracles. I could find you the names."

"Good. In the meantime, have you called the police?"

"They know about this Satan. Years ago a nursing home I owned in Hyde Park burned down. The same week the hostage rescue in Tehran failed. A very terrible fire. Thank the heavens the building was closed for renovation work. A gasoline tank next door exploded, a fireman was killed. Half a million dollars damage."

"And it was arson."

"Oh yes. Mrs. O'Hare managed the nursing home for me, and just before the fire a threat came to her on the phone."

"The cops will wonder why you didn't warn her this time."

"Dorothy opened the mail here, she knew. I found these notes on her desk." He flung his hand toward the fireplace, where turbaned hunters and a panther were stalking each other on a silky carpet. "Mr. Ames, you could walk outside your door on the finest sunny day, and—"

He smacked his hands together with a crack that sounded like Sari's toy pistol. I knew what he meant. Look under a toadstool in the land of the free and the home of the brave, and the elf may be packing a mail-order .38.

"Someone's threatening your life," I said. "You go to the police. Step one."

"I call you," he insisted. "Step two."

"What do you want me to do?"

"Make things secure in my house. Send me the bill."

"First," I said, "call a state police lieutenant named Auburn. He's handling the O'Hare murder."

"You think it was this Satan?"

"It's possible. It was a kind of execution."

I sketched in the picture. Mehdi Farhat squeezed his

eyes shut with sympathy and distaste. But he kept his head: "Tomorrow I want you to look over my doors and my cars and my office. Make a list. Buy whatever locks you think."

"Tomorrow's Sunday."

"Satans don't care about Sunday."

Chapter Eight

Meg was feeling better and worse on Sunday. Less painkiller, more reality. With her jaw wired she seemed to be muttering through clenched teeth: "Duncan, shtop shtaring."

"I'm just keeping you company."

"It makesh me feel like such a bashket case. Sho dependent on you."

"It was a traffic accident. You got totaled by a drunk priest from Framingham. Not your fault. Relax."

"I hate it."

Her unbandaged eye glared at me. I was going to jump on her about her attitude, but I thought, what the hell. The news that she'd lost an eye had knocked the spirit out of her. I sat by her bed, not saying much. Once or twice I got her some ice water which she sucked through a pleated straw. "Got a itch," she murmured. "Could you rub my nose a widdle?"

My nose began to tickle in sympathy, and I ended up rubbing both at once. I'd known Meg a long time.

Her gaze shifted to the IV bottle at the end of its plastic umbilicus as if she still couldn't imagine how she'd gotten here. Outside the window the city hovered in the dazzling

May sunlight. After a while her eyelid fluttered and she slept. I may have dozed too, because suddenly I was aware of someone watching me from the doorway.

Dr. Schell.

For a little privacy we strolled up and down the corridor with Styrofoam cups of tea, discussing medicine and hate mail. Carol knew nothing about the satanic notes sent to Dr. Farhat.

"Mehdi should've gone to the police," she said bitterly. "Maybe it would've scared off this nut."

"Your mother knew about the threats. But she ignored them. Just as she did before the nursing-home fire."

"God, I'd forgotten the fire." The connection excited her. "Whoever the threatening caller was, my mother was totally pigheaded about it. She started telling him off over the phone."

"And?"

"Guy hung up. Next evening it was like a bomb went off, and the old place burned right to the ground."

"She had nerve, your mother."

"She also loved that job. She was her own boss there, and the money was good. The threat made her mad, as if it was just the neighborhood she grew up in trying to beat her out of her success." Carol crushed her plastic cup and deftly tossed it into a plastic-lined waste hamper behind the nurses' desk. She frowned. "Maybe I should buy a pistol."

"Pistols kill more neighbors than burglars."

"Mother's funeral is tomorrow. I'm going to feel I'm being watched the whole time."

"Perhaps I should be there."

"I'd be"—she gave an awkward shrug—"glad."

That afternoon I went through Mehdi Farhat's place making security notes. I phoned New York and asked Vera to send him a copy of our pamphlet on safety precautions for business folks. The pamphlet was one-third common sense and two-thirds juju, but the terrorist tattle on the airwaves had a lot of people jumpy. Since the US raid on Libya our pamphlet had been a best seller.

Mehdi gave me the names of several worrisome patients. One had tried to trick him into falsifying insurance forms: a Patrick Shaughnessy of Charlestown. They'd skirmished over the matter and Mehdi had let it drop. Then one night a year or so ago Shaughnessy had phoned from a bar in a drunken tantrum. Mehdi called the cops.

On the way out I looked into the barn in back, where Olaf Thorsson's antique fire engines sat. Thorsson had made some of his loot in insurance, and he'd begun his hobby as an advertising gimmick. There were a horse-drawn steamer, a tubby pumper, a ladder truck very like the one in a book I had as a kid, and a couple other old heroes. They sat in the dusky barn, smelling of grease and stale leather, waiting for a call to save civilization.

Chapter Nine

Pat Shaughnessy worked at the Waltham-Route 128 terminal of Foxx New England, the interstate trucker. Monday morning I found him on the warehouse dock: a guy in his forties, built like the forklift truck he was driving. For twenty minutes I watched him loading a trailer, admiring his skill. The forklift wheeled about, juggling heavy skid pallets with an elephant's impossible grace. Finally he took a break.

"They send you out here to spy on us? There's nothing in the contract about spying on the dockhands."

I flashed my ID. "I'm an investigator."

"That ain't no FBI shield." His face reminded me of Long John Silver in the movie. A mean sort of cockiness in the eyes—although I don't recall Long John using a crew cut to combat hair loss. "If you got questions about the box they hijacked in March, you better ask in the office for—"

"Were you involved?"

"Hell no. That rig disappeared in the middle of the night. Locks and all. It was parked right over there, full of liquor."

"You own a pistol?"

"What do I need with that shit? I can take care of myself. Give me a chair like they do lions with."

"Where were you last Thursday after work?"

"Who wants to know?"

I took a chance: "Dorothy O'Hare."

"And who might that be?"

"She worked for a chiropractor who treated you once."

"If that asshole sent you to collect his bill, forget it. You can tell him, he hounds me, I squawk about those insurance forms."

"What insurance forms?"

"Don't give me that shit. The insurance forms he wants you to file so he can grab the payoff."

"How many times did he treat you?"

"How many hairs on the pope's ass?"

"Two times? Twenty?"

"A million is more like it. Rubbing you with his fingers. He gets off on that."

"Did it help?"

"If you can stand up after a day on this job, after all the lifting and shit, you got a fence post up your ass."

"Where were you Thursday night?"

"How come you ask so many questions?"

"Can you prove where you were?"

"Can you talk without your teeth?"

"Should I ask the cops instead?"

"You should mind your own business."

"Something I shouldn't know about?"

"Mind your own fucking business."

"Needle's stuck on your record."

As I turned to go the forklift whined into action. He had a light touch. Before I thought to dodge, one fork had pinned me against a wooden crate, chest high, face-to-face with cartons labeled "FRAGILE: HANDLE WITH CARE." I sucked in a breath. I remembered how Japanese beetles snap under kids' sneakers. Pat Shaughnessy was looking into the distance, watching out for witnesses. "You come around threatening people," he said, "and you get hurt. You'll need more than a fucking fairy back massage, understand?"

"I see your point."

The forklift backed off.

I decided to keep an open mind about Pat Shaughnessy.

Chapter Ten

By the time I reached the Feeney Funeral Home in Hyde Park the O'Hare party had already moved on. A freckled maiden with Ireland still under her tongue stopped vacuuming long enough to direct me to St. Michael's Church. I felt a ridiculous stab of guilt. Late again. It was the second time I'd let Dorothy down.

The church glistened with fresh gilt and flowers. Carol sat grimly beside Mehdi Farhat. There was a scattering of old dears and a number of younger women who I later learned had served with Dorothy in various civic organizations. No sign of Jerry the Ex.

A monsignor did the honors, assisted by a quartet of altar boys and a taped soprano voice singing modish arias with an easy-listening feel. The monsignor hoped we would never forget that Dorothy had learned the mysteries of eternal love in a soundly supported parochial school, and would have wanted all of us, and our children, and their children too, to have the same blessing. Let us remember our responsibility to give.

The trip to the cemetery featured a taped carillon playing the triumphal march from Handel's *Judas Maccabeus* which I remembered from Rachel's Suzuki fiddle lessons years ago. They set up the coffin beside the grave, keeping the everlasting hole itself covered with Astroturf. I thought of those traps the Vietcong dug that strewed vegetation over a hole spiked with punji sticks to impale visitors.

During the closing ceremonies I stood next to Dorothy's tubby and frankly gray sister. Gladys Clancy had remained Hyde Park Irish. "Who'd of thought," she murmured to me. "As kids Dot was always sticking up for me. Somebody'd give me a hard time and Dot would go after them like gangbusters and come back bawling with a bloody nose."

Mr. Clancy said, "It was you did the bawling after Dot sold the old lady's house right out from under your nose."

Mr. Clancy had the red-faced bluntness of a retired construction worker and the body of a kodiak bear. The rear window of his Buick Skylark dangled a yellow diamond sign that read: "Sexy Senior Citizen on Board." He was holding his sporty plaid cap and staring into the distance as if he hadn't said a thing. Gladys protested: "That was that lawyer did that."

"That was your sister stealing the eyes out of your head."

"Don't mock the departed," Gladys crooned. And to me: "There was misunderstandings about how my mother's estate was to be divided. But like I say, with Dot being on her own all her married life, you couldn't begrudge her a little something."

"So long as you didn't have to see the parties she threw for her big-shot friends in Newton."

Mrs. C kept compromising: "She loved a good time, Dot did."

Mr. C stared at the spring clouds as if speaking his mind directly to his heaven-bound sister-in-law: "Gladys just got over the shingles. You have any idea how many copayments that means?"

Before I could guess Carol came over. Up close, in her eyes, she looked sick. A little bit destroyed. With a squeeze of the hand she thanked me for coming. Mrs. C bubbled gently while her husband turned his plaid cap round and round in his hands as if worried that Carol's suffering might be contagious.

Five years before Pat Shaughnessy had clobbered a guy with a bar stool in Charlestown and strolled away from a manslaughter rap. Plea of self-defense, case continued without a finding. Every Irish aunt in Charlestown must have scratched hard to hire the lawyer.

The Boston cop who'd handled the case shared my feeling that Pat Shaughnessy might be an occasional mad dog in your local saloon, but wasn't a killer by temperament.

As for the nursing-home investigation: like the fire itself, the case had finally burned out. Nobody showed much interest in sifting the ashes at this late date. The state cop, Phil Auburn, had a lot of evil competing for his attention. Looking over his notebook like a racing form, he tried to pick the surest winners.

On my own I found the Arab-American Anti-Discrimination League. Mrs. Baroodi, the secretary, was my age, a serious woman with keen eyes and a shadow of mustache on her lip. "Yes, yes," she encouraged me, "it's terrorism of course. Just like against the Jews and everybody else. Eighteen months ago our Southern California director was killed by a bomb. No arrests. There's so much prejudice against Arabs that sometimes you wonder if the police half bother to investigate these attacks. I could show you file after file."

In the typewriter behind her was testimony her boss planned to deliver before the House subcommittee on criminal justice.

"Got any Satans in your files?" I asked. We both looked at the steel file cabinet by the window.

"We've got all kinds. The only problem is, we don't know many of their street addresses." Mrs. Baroodi didn't laugh. "But I can tell you one of the big haters around here. He owns an electronics supply house in Belmont, and puts out this trash."

From the file she pulled a newspaper titled *Heritage Strike Force*. The contents:

> Jew Spies Sap Pentagon Strength
> Haitians, Puerto Ricans and AIDS
> Corporal Punishment Improves Black IQs
> Arab Terrorists Soon to Have A-Weapons

The editorial had the hot urgency of intestinal flu:

> White Americans are in danger of Extinction. In the Third World, birth rates are 200% higher than for US. It is a well-known law of science that insects and rats reproduce faster than the higher animals with bigger brains. Every immigrant who spawns a family in US is a cancer cell fed by Communist poisons. Concerned citizens should compile lists of sites where these cancers grow so they can be surgically removed from US before time runs out. Support the right to bear arms, not the welfare state . . .

The editorial marched on, commanding me to defend myself and the holy ovaries in my harem. Unlike white supremacists such as Posse Comitatus, this crusade carefully neglected to call for the overthrow of the U.S. Constitution.

Mrs. Baroodi said, "A man named Donald Frazier puts out this newspaper several times a year."

"Is he as violent in life as he is in print?"

"We have our suspicions. We'd like to see his mailing list."

"I wonder if he knows our Mr. Satan."

"You may have to go through hell to find out."

I didn't laugh, but then neither did she.

Belmont, the town that gave us the John Birch Society once upon a time, is one of those suburbs that have been digested into the sprawl of greater Boston. F & F Electronics fortified itself in a one-story cinder-block building between a hardware store and a discount drug outlet. The sign advertised security systems, and F & F practiced what it preached. The door sported multiple locks. Bars and alarm tape adorned the windows.

The racks inside displayed audio and automotive gear as well as electric eyes, alarms, and CB radios. On the counter sat leaflets inviting me to a slide presentation explaining "The IQ Test Conspiracy." A sign commanded me to "Take One." I obeyed.

It was May yet the guy by the cash register wore a plaid flannel shirt. He was bald with a friar's fringe of black hair. Not fat but chipmunk-pouchy, with purplish lips and suspicious eyes. Make that fanatic eyes. His hands were stripping antenna leads on the counter. He didn't say hello, he just sized me up.

"Help you?"

"I'm looking for the publisher of *Heritage Strike Force*."

"I'm Don Frazier. You like what you read?"

"I only look at the pictures."

"There aren't any pic—who are you, anyway?"

"You're acquainted with the Arab-American Anti-Discrimination League."

"So what."

"One of your readers wants to see their Boston office remodeled." I lit an invisible fuse and put my fingers in my ears. He got the idea.

"A bomb?"

I kept a straight face. "My man will provide raw materials and pay for the delivery."

"You got the wrong guy."

"My man thinks you know the right guy."

"That depends." He pretended to study his wristwatch, an impressive silver model with space-cadet dials. I said, "The magic name is the American Satan."

Mr. Frazier stared at the wristwatch, debating with himself, as if we were waiting for a computer to crunch the data. Then a little red light went on in his brain: "I'll tell you what I think. I think you're trying to set me up."

"Just give me Satan's phone number. You don't have to be involved at all."

"What I think is, you're from the FBI and . . ."

I shrugged. "Let's let Satan decide that."

"Or Bureau of Alcohol and Firearms, or whatever."

"It's okay, be cautious. That's what we want, not some half-assed nut. Let's bring the roof down on them, not on us."

He was splitting the antenna's wire leads with a penknife: "You people ought to use the government's force against real enemies instead of threatening the people who want to wake this country up."

I leaned over the counter: "You set the terms. We're on your side, and the price is right."

"There's laws against entrapment." He glared at me. I watched his hands. Doughty merchants like Don Frazier tend to keep a fowling piece behind the counter. Anger was crowding the worry out of his eyes: "I don't play games."

"I'll leave you a phone number in case you turn up a Satan for me."

"I don't know any Satan. I'm not into secret code names and childish crap like that. I don't have—this country doesn't have enough time. The world's getting too crowded for that. With this trillion-dollar debt, you got aliens taking over the country. Jobs, banks, publishers, everything."

I sympathized: "Good. You're our man."

He studied the wire he was slicing, lips pinched tight in concentration, as if not listening. *"Heritage* stands for the power of rational choice over animalism, and I resent—"

"Stay in touch."

He was still standing up for Reason as I went out the door.

Chapter Eleven

Vera phoned from New York, spiky with frustration. "What's going on up there? I expected you back in the office today. I'm your partner not your answering service. That photo store in Brooklyn is after you about the—"

"Meg's a mess." I ran through the list of medical horrors.

Vera groaned in sympathy, then: "And why didn't you ring me up?"

"I need to keep an eye on Rachel at least till her mother's out of the hospital. I've been studying your expense-account program on the computer. It's brilliant."

"Oh rubbish."

"And I seem to be involved in a murder investigation." I told her about the soupy fate of Dorothy O'Hare. I downplayed Carol's role in my decision by not mentioning her. Vera is a scrappy export of Huddersfield England, where most of her pals were sleepwalking through forced unemployment. In ten years in New York she'd studied computer lingos at CCNY and dirty business in ninety-nine different jobs. We liked working together well enough not to take it for granted.

"It's all well and good for you to go larking around with murdered old ladies, but—"

"Don't be jealous."

"Jealous? I should say not. I just don't want you billing the firm for your bloody holiday."

"You're a slave driver, Vee."

"Remember the phone number here, will you?"

"Speaking of which. Today I gave the off-line office number to a guy who's involved with hate organizations. I'm trying to recruit him to bomb the office of an Arab lobbying group in Boston. If a Donald Frazier calls, ask how I make the contact. Don't let him fish out of you who we are."

"For God's sake, Duncan. Don't get hurt. Just because the insurance people employ us now and then doesn't mean they're on our side. And you're not thirty-nine anymore, love."

"Happy birthday to you, too."

"You know what I mean."

"Why don't you come up to Boston for a few days so I can breathe tender trifles in your ear."

"Because my partner's blown off and left me stranded here with all the work, is why."

"The cad. Give him a piece of your mind. Even better, give him a piece of your—"

"What was that last word?"

"Bad connection. I'll call you tonight."

"Ha. Phone sex. How low can we sink?"

Rachel was beginning to get on my case. Before the divorce she'd waged the usual teenage war of liberation, but mostly against her mother. The divorce made me the adversary. Worse than being oppressed by parents, she decided, was being abandoned by one. So now she preferred to ambush me.

As we pulled into Francis Street by the hospital Tuesday afternoon, I spotted Carol Schell's BMW double-parked. Carol waved. "Okay, kid," I said, "I'll pick you up around six."

Rachel balked: "Aren't you coming in to see Mom?"

"First I have to discuss some things with Dr. Schell. She's expecting me."

"You like her, don't you." An accusation.

"You don't?"

"She ignores me."

"Carol's got a lot on her mind."

"And she's a snob."

"Oh?"

"It's just too neat, that BMW she drives. And the vinyl cover over the front to keep insects from yukking up the paint. Do you know what that thing is called?"

"A car like that costs money. You protect it."

"It's called 'Le Bra.' Can you believe that? A bra for your car. Doesn't she even realize the stereotype junk women are trying to escape from?"

"The cover probably keeps the radiator running hotter in winter."

"Oh Dad, come off it. It's *May*. I mean, have a heart, that's Barbie-doll crap. I bet her apartment is the Barbie Dream House." Rachel gave a superior snort that swept Dr. C into the trash can of history.

"She's my client."

"Oh sure."

"Don't be so jealous."

"Well, I don't want to wait around for you all night in the hospital. I wish I had a car. Mom's Ford got totaled in the accident. When do we buy a new one?"

"Don't worry, I'll stick around a while longer."

"What good is that? You hog the car."

"I won't leave you stranded."

"Oh brother," she grumbled. "Where have I heard that before."

Her eyes said *Checkmate*.

Chapter Twelve

"Should I be afraid of this Satan nut?" Carol asked. We were eating pocket sandwiches at a quick-lunch joint down the street from Symphony Hall. I felt smug eating a veggie sandwich, skip the mayo, with a tennis-playing doctor in a spandex sports bra. Yet her face still had the bleak, scrubbed look it had at the funeral. Shadows under the eyes, slack in the chops. Maybe she'd be one of those golden girls who suddenly turn ashen in middle age. "It's getting on my nerves," she sighed. "I sit down in my apartment and I have the sensation someone's there behind me. And of course, stupid me, I look."

I shrugged. "I'm not sure how to read those satanic notes. They're almost too helpful."

"You think they're just crank notes?"

"I wish I knew. Why attack a nice old lady named O'Hare if it's Iran you hate? I'd feel better if there'd been some raping and looting, not just a clean send-off."

"The police say only a fraction of these random house-break-type murders are ever solved."

"Maybe it won't turn out to be so random after all."

"Think they'll figure it out?"

"Look. Your mother was more or less executed. She

must have been upright when the pistol went off behind her. Yet the onion soup hardly spattered."

"She fell forward very slowly."

"Or someone grabbed her by the hair, fired, then put her head down."

Carol's eyes wobbled, she seemed about to gag. I put my hand on her wrist:

"Take it easy."

Her eyes were streaming: "God, I hate that acid taste."

"Here, drink some water."

"Ever since med school my stomach's been a mess. Too much garlic in this sandwich, too." The color came back into her face. "It's strange, I can stand blood and gore—in Emergency I can stitch up big ragged holes in people—but add the idea of violence and I fall apart. I have this gunshot case now, Tony. Somebody shot him in a men's room about three blocks from here. A dope pusher, hardly old enough for a driver's license. His abdomen's perforated like—"

I changed the subject: "Your mother ever mention a Pat Shaughnessy?" She shook her head. "How about the name Donald Frazier? Or a publication called *Heritage Strike Force*?"

"Uh-uh."

"How about Jerry Schell?"

"That's my husband. Ex-husband. Are you teasing me?"

"I've been talking to him. He's happy to have a dead mother-in-law. And he has no alibi."

"Come on, Duncan. All Jerry cares about is money. Paper empires."

"I'd like to know where Jerry was when your mother sat down to dine."

"What you mean is, you want me to try to find out."

"I'd like to put my mind at ease."

"God, you're serious about Jerry, aren't you?"

"Let me know what you find out. Maybe we can compare diagnoses over dinner. Professional consultation."

"You know, I really can't pay you for your work."

"I can quit when I like."

"The other night I had a crazy thought that it was you who killed my mother. That's how paranoid I've been."

"Sorry to hear it."

"I don't want to hate you."

"I'll do what I can to prevent it."

Chapter Thirteen

Next morning I stopped into the Covenant Press in Watertown, which prints *Heritage Strike Force*. Convenant's president and number-one salesman, Norman Forrest, was a tall, boyish enthusiast, feathery gray above the ears. With a little encouragement, he mistook me for an insurance investigator.

"Mr. Frazier's a good account. He pays his bills on time. Not that I like the guff he puts out. Frankly, we're happier doing stockholders' reports for the Shawmut Bank."

"Who writes his stuff?"

"I'd guess he generates most of the copy himself. He's a little paranoid about my typesetters tampering with his words. Got a bug about being censored. Every time he comes in he jokes about using a modem so his Radio Shack computer at home can directly feed into our computer-typesetting operation."

"Do you do Mr. Frazier's mailing for him?"

"We could. But most of his print run is giveaways. And his home computer has a mail-merge program for labeling the pieces he mails."

"Ever hear him use the phrase 'the American Satan'?"

"That sounds like Communist talk. Is Frazier in trouble with the government?"

Norman looked concerned. Phineas L. Forrest, "Founder of the Covenant Press, Inc. 1877–1926," watched us from a sepia-toned photo on the office wall. Phineas was politely choking to death in his starched collar, and he didn't approve of what he saw.

Don Frazier lived in a grim green ranch house off Trapelo Road in Waltham. Chopped box of a place with an anonymous yard, like a 1950s motel. Treeless too: perhaps for a cleaner field of fire when the apocalyptic niggers and spics finally launched their human-wave assault on the Fraziers' master bedroom.

The last time Vera had called a computer repairman into the office, the guy had turned up in banker's duds with a little leather tool kit, so I wore my silk necktie and toted my briefcase as I headed up Frazier's walk.

Before my finger could punch the bell the door jerked open. Mrs. Frazier was a sharp-nosed brunette maybe ten years younger than her husband. Her hairdo curled at the edges like the flounce on a sofa. She had a red-nosed cold which intensified the impression of mousey bleariness. Under her arm, as if to beat a leaky dog, she carried a rolled-up magazine.

"I saw you come up the walk," she explained. "My kids just fell asleep. We got colds, all of us. Don's not here."

"I know, I saw him at the store. I have to check out his computer." This was true and not true. She frowned so I added, "Have to see if I can hook up his computer to run the typesetting program at Covenant Press. He wants to press a button here and have it turn directly into a million printed copies."

She groaned: "I just got Ryan and Sean to sleep."

"I won't make a sound." I raised my briefcase and put my finger to my lips. "What are you reading?"

She unfolded a magazine called *Self*. "It's got this diet, the longevity diet, that we're on. It really works."

"So I see."

"You can tell?"

"Sure. You're not dead."

"Oh. I thought you meant I looked, you know, svelte."

"You do."

"Nice-looking tie you got. Good cloth. I like the little gold arrows. Very rich-looking. Where'd you buy it?"

"My daughter gave it to me."

"You don't have a cigarette, do you?"

"No such luck."

"Well, come on in. I can't stand here, my program's on."

Frazier had an office space laid out on a pea-green shag carpet in the cellar. His computer keyboard sat in a rolltop desk of unfinished pine, the monitor perched above. The raw pine had grown dingy gray. A table improvised from a luan door held neat piles of clippings from newspapers, the John Birch Society, American Nazis, and various TV evangelists. Between two file cabinets stood back issues of *Heritage Strike Force* in tidy stacks. I flipped on the computer and hunted for diskettes. Maybe I was going to get a break.

Maybe not.

Every file I tapped spilled old rant of Frazier's onto the green screen, but no mailing list. No Satans. Then Mrs. F was on the stairs behind me. "You're not smoking, are you? Don doesn't allow smoke in the house. I thought I smelled something."

Her nose twitched. A mouse on the stairs. She sneezed. I tried another diskette. Up came a ditty about the Nicaraguan Contras as saviors of Judeo-Christian culture as we know it.

A door slammed upstairs.

"Oh," peeped the mouse. "Here's Don now."

As I exited the program, Mrs. Mouse scuttered up to the Mr. His voice barked, hers peeped, I slipped out the cellar door. The steel bulkhead creaked loudly on its hinges. When I stepped out onto the grass, Frazier was on the back porch with a nickel-plated pistol in both hands, his body crouched in varsity gunfighter position. As Grandma Ames would say, he was fit to be tied.

I waved. "Hello, young lovers."

"Don't move. Debbie, call the cops."

Debbie looked out the kitchen door, missing her program. I walked around to the steps and started up. Frazier warned me back. Debbie echoed him: "You heard him, go back."

I didn't.

"So it's you," Frazier said. He was again wearing a plaid flannel shirt with a pocketful of ballpoint pens and a woodsman's compass clipped to his belt. Deerslayer, ready to take on the wilderness. He kept wagging the pistol at me.

It seemed like a good time for a change of tactics. "Tell me the truth and you can still get out of this unscathed."

"You're the one in trouble, asshole."

"Personally, I think you're innocent. But if you want to discuss it with every cop east of Pittsburgh, dial 911."

"Innocent of what! That's a God damned lie."

"I won't ask if you have a permit for the weapon."

"You bet your God damned—"

"It figures."

I brushed the snubby gun barrel aside, watching the muscles in his face for warning signs. To cover his submission he pretended to wipe sweat off his bald forehead. While he kept his monkish fringe cropped close, he allowed himself sideburns. Come to think of it, he had a dimple in his upper lip and big boyish ears. It was the eyes that worried me.

Debbie was hanging on the door frame listening. I took a chance. "You're implicated in a murder, Mr. Frazier."

"What?" A plaintive note complicated his indignation.

"The American Satan. You told me the other day that name means nothing to you."

"Nothing. Triple zero."

"Suppose I offer you a polygraph test to prove it."

"Look. All I do is write articles. I got First Amendment protection. The First Amendment specifically reads—"

"A woman's dead," I said. "The net is going out in your direction. You willing to do a polygraph for us or not?"

"What do I have to hide? Zero." His face was white as a Klansman's sheet. "I mean, nothing. Triple zero."

"Then you won't mind donating some truth to the cause."

His voice quavered: "I'll be there."

"Tomorrow morning. Nine sharp."

"I have a right to couns—"

"The idea is to act quietly and fast, before the official wheels start grinding you up. Don't quote me."

"I'm not giving up my rights."

"A man of principles. Good for you. And good luck."

As I turned to go he blurted, "Hey, wait. I didn't say no, did I?"

"Tomorrow morning. Nine sharp. You can make it?"

"I said I would."

I gave him a Soul-Searching Stare. "Okay. I'll make my report very favorable. If the polygraph is still necessary, I'll phone you."

"What about the murder? What's this murder?"

"I can't prejudice the case," I said.

"What about your name? What outfit—?"

"You don't want to know any more than you have to, Mr. Frazier. Take my word for it."

Chapter Fourteen

Meg was cranked up in the bed for the first time. Bandages still covered the bad eye and part of her jaw. "Hey," I called, "don't you look lively today. Carol tells me you're off baby food now."

"Carol?"

"Dr. Schell."

"Aren't we chummy."

"Is that jealousy I hear?"

"She'sh all right. Who shent the flowersh?"

She indicated the vase of exuberant blossoms that had shown up beside her bed courtesy of Dr. Mehdi Farhat. I was filling her in on the donor when she cut me off:

"Duncan, I'm shcared. Rachel wantsh to go to Nicaragua. With the Quakersh. To help poor farmersh and shick babies."

"Good for her."

"She'sh a kid. From a shilly suburb."

"Even suburban brats can grow up."

"They'll kill her."

"The farmers won't hurt her."

"There'sh a war down there. The CIA ones, the Contra'sh, they'll kill anyone. They don't care."

"It scares me too. But I trust her more than I trust most people with green hair. She wants her life to mean something."

"She'sh getting back at me," Meg insisted. "I pushed that shummer job on her. It sheemed perfect."

The perfect job meant videotaping rich people's valuables for insurance purposes. I shrugged: "Rachel thinks the job's obscene. Her word."

"But she *lovesh* to use the video camera. And it *paysh*. What a fool I am."

"Nobody's perfect."

"I know," she said gloomily. "I saw myself in the mirror this afternoon. I look dead."

"It's only temporary."

"Are you temporary too?"

"I can stick around a while longer. But Vera needs me."

"Oh." Meg was flustered. "If you have to go, go. We'll make out. Only, please . . . talk to Rachel."

"Sure." I gave her a squeeze. "But trust her."

"I'd rather have all my bonesh broken than have to worry about my kid like thish. You know?"

The cops seemed to be in no hurry to check on Jerry Schell's whereabouts at the time his mother-in-law was slipping into her soup, so the job fell to the private sector.

He owned a newly renovated condo on Melrose Street in the South End, where Boston's movie distributors are clustered, a shout away from the Combat Zone. His neighbors were impeccable minders of their own business, and told me so. With one exception, a young professor named Beaton. I'd been meeting such resistance that I switched to a less direct approach.

"Does the upstairs doorbell work? I was here looking

for Jerry Schell last Thursday night, and nobody answered."

First the Beatons were stymied, then they remembered that around eight-thirty on Thursday—it was just dark—they'd followed Jerry's car around and around the block searching for a parking space.

They were pleased that when I rang the bell now, Jerry's voice answered in the croaky intercom. I shot upstairs.

Nice place. A wall or two had gone bye-bye to make room for teak furniture, stereo speakers the size of coffins, and a Persian rug plush enough for contact sports. A coolie-hat lampshade hovered over a coffee table cluttered with loose-leaf binders, record jackets, a couple bottles of Samuel Adams beer, and two plates smelling of clam sauce. My attorney had company.

"Larry and I are doing some figures. I don't have much time."

Jerry himself was in his stocking feet wearing jeans and a Bruce Springsteen T-shirt. Larry slouched in a beanbag chair, dirty blond, barefoot, and vaguely illegal. On the other hand, his strawberry-red velveteen slacks and matching sailor's shirt couldn't have been more fastidious. Facially he resembled James Dean or a Polish plumber I'd once had as a client, depending on the angle. Jerry was eager to hear about the investigation.

"So what the hell do you want?"

"I'm worried about you. You weren't home last Thursday night. You told me a fib."

"Funny man." He grimaced. "Who's put you up to this? Who are you, anyway?"

"I am the angel Duncan. Sent from on high. I implore you to repent. If you're not guilty, I urge you to prove it before the temporal powers kick your ass."

"The angel Duncan. I like that." Jerry Schell smiled. The helpful Larry said, "What an imagination. Who's programmed this guy?"

I gave Jerry Schell my attention. "The cops are going to ask. Where were you when your mother-in-law's lights went out?"

"In the dark."

Larry laughed, a hacking gurgle that cried out for the Heimlich maneuver. Jerry Schell recovered some of his confidence.

"Out, angel. Out." He jerked his thumb like an umpire.

"You own a pistol?"

"Out!"

Larry horselaughed, the near-hysterical merriment that comes out of backwoods Colombia in powder form. "Shall I put him out?" he offered. His strawberry-red sailor shirt advertised manly biceps. He came at me, bare feet sinking in the carpet.

"Slow down," I said. "I'm an old man."

"Bull," said Larry. But he hesitated.

"Why are you harassing me like this?" Jerry Schell pouted. "Who's paying you?"

In the world of Jerry the Wonderlawyer only money talked. I said, "Bullet blows brains out. Hostile relative lacks alibi. Problem."

"Hostile my fucking ass."

Larry and his host exchanged tense looks. All over my body muscles were preparing for strenuous exercise. I said, "Sooner or later you'll have more to say."

Larry grabbed the knot of my tie. "Out you go."

I put my foot down where his toes happened to be. He yelled, releasing my necktie in a prompt and courteous manner. He didn't accompany me to the staircase.

Chapter Fifteen

Rachel said, "Your chiropractor called. I told him you were working on his problem, but he wasn't real happy."

When I called Mehdi Farhat the next morning, he complained, "I need you. I signed a contract. Where have you been?"

"I've been busy eliminating American Satans."

He snorted so feelingly into the phone that I felt like his handkerchief. "You missed one. Another threat came."

"Same message?"

" 'Stop cops,' it says. 'Stop cops or the end.' We better tell the police to stay away. Forget this whole thing."

"How does he know you've been to the cops?"

"Obviously he spies on me. And you should stay away too. It's not worth it. I'll send you your last check."

"I'm involved."

"No, no. It's too dangerous for me."

"I'll stay away from you."

"You'll get me killed."

"I won't contact you at all."

"But I want to know what have you found out. Anything?"

I gave him a streamlined report on my visits with

Shaughnessy and Don Frazier. "I don't know about Shaughnessy, but Frazier's willing to take a polygraph test. So I'm inclined to rule him out."

"This Shaughnessy ran up a big treatment bill, then acted like a stupid donkey about paying."

"But I don't think he's the literary type."

"How much brain is needed to glue newspaper words? How much brain is needed to pull a trigger?"

As we headed toward Boston on Route 9 in the Volvo, Rachel asked, "What newspaper did this Satan cut his words out of?"

"You're into art and design. Find out for me."

"If you make me Xeroxes, I can compare them to the type fonts of the *Globe* and like that."

I gave her my blessing, pulling off in Newton Highlands. "I want to ask Dorothy O'Hare's neighbors a question or two."

Rachel didn't object. In fact she went with me from house to house ringing doorbells the way we used to do when I was a Cub Scout selling Baby Ruths and Almond Joys to buy Red Sox tickets, in the days before parents worried about the neighbors killing kids.

In the bay-windowed house across the street from Dorothy O'Hare's, a hawk-eyed granny named Mary Day was happy to talk to us through her locked screen door. She remembered the widow and her little girl moving into that big house the fall those people landed on the moon. A rented trailer on the back bumper, that was all they had. The girl was a doctor now, but you'd never have guessed it seeing how fresh she was then, sassing her mother, lighting candles under the porch—one time they nearly burned down the garage, her and those fresh kids. The mother was always having to whale the tar out of her. Like the time she cut the flowers in everybody's gardens and then went door-to-door selling people their own flowers. Mr. Day lost his temper. Not that she paid him any mind. Sharp as a tack, she was. Always on the honor roll. And pretty, too. Goldilocks, Mr. Day used to call her. Goldilocks.

"But the night Mrs. O'Hare was murdered, you didn't notice anything odd."

"I wouldn't unlock my door after that. Not if the President himself came here to see my embroidery."

"But Thursday night you didn't see anybody strange," Rachel prompted.

"No, just the husband. He drove her home."

"I thought she was a widow," Rachel said.

"No no no. The daughter's husband. Carol's. He drove Mrs. O'Hare home in his silver car."

"Jerry Schell? You're sure it was his car?"

"Oh my, yes. My son Craig has one the exact same color, but without the wires on the wheels. Like the old roadsters used to have. You wouldn't remember those."

"Did Schell go into the house?"

"I didn't spy on them. I try to keep abreast of things but I'm not nosy."

"How long did the car stay?"

"Not long. *Wheel of Fortune* was on TV. When I looked again he'd driven away."

"Less than half an hour."

"I didn't see Carol this time."

"They're divorced," I said.

"Wouldn't you know." Mrs. Day's mouth formed a wistful but critical knot. "It's a lot easier for women now than it was in my day. Let me tell you."

"Have you told the police any of this?"

"Not really. I was napping when they came by. My son Craig talked to them."

I slipped my card through the door and invited her to keep remembering.

"Well, I do recall the time the girl got a prize from Jordan Marsh for the best Easter dress, and she was in the newspaper. I suppose the mother must have made it. All white lace with little blue flowers and a whole—"

"You have an astounding memory."

"I'm sorry Craig's not home so's you could come in."

Going back to the car, Rachel let my hand hitch a ride on her shoulder. She said, "Your doctor friend sounds like she was more fun as a kid."

Tree shadows striped the sidewalk and the afternoon sun knifed across the lawns and the radioactive spring flower beds. On the wooded hill behind the O'Hare house the bricks of a school glowed dusky red. Pigeons roosted in the fancy Victorian eaves. It was getting late. The sun stabbed under porches and shrubs and cars at an angle that reminded you of wintry afternoons in childhood and the sudden urge to rush indoors for supper, out of the freezing dusk.

Carol came into Meg's room to brief her on the surgery scheduled for her left eye. Through a gap in the skimpy curtain I watched her perch on the edge of Meg's bed with her clipboard, translating the medical hocus-pocus. Toes touching the floor, Carol half leaned against the bed, pen to her lips, reddish goldilocks springy around her ears. As a doctor she was a lot more sympathetic than some of the professional egos you meet doing malpractice work.

"Once you adjust," I heard her saying, "you'll see more

with one eye than most people do with two. Your depth perception won't be as good, that's all."

"I'll like shallow people more," Meg joked.

"And there'll be more people to like."

"I could play golf?"

"You could do anything but shoot flies with a BB gun."

"My secret wish."

"Mine too."

"Why am I worried?"

Carol touched her shoulder: "I'll be there with you."

Dr. C finished her rounds by examining the drug dealer who'd been shot up on Mission Hill. Tony D'Agostino was Rachel's age, proud of his biceps and his wounds and the diamond twinkling in his right earlobe. With his dark, curly-headed good looks and his tendency to pose, Tony could have been riding a dolphin in a Roman mosaic.

"Hey, Dr. Fox," he teased. "Come over here, I got my ice on today. Inspect it real close."

"Uh-uh. I'm wise to you."

"Hey, like, no kisses this time. That was just a token of my esteem. Come on," he coaxed, "let's do some weed, make your heart beat."

"Not today, lover."

"You give me a shot, I give you one."

"You'll be going home soon."

"Then we got to party now."

"Not today, lover."

"Who's that in the doorway? Your husband?"

Carol shot a flustered glance at me: "None of your business, Tony."

Afterward I walked her down to Radiology.

"Did you find out where Jerry was Thursday night?"

She stepped up her pace. "I haven't seen Jerry. To be perfectly honest, I'd go out of my way to avoid him."

"When I talk to him he has a forked tongue."

She was just about skipping down the corridor now. "I know you think you're being helpful—"

"Slow down."

"This is a hospital," she said coolly, "not obedience training."

"Listen to me. Jerry drove your mother home. Just before her date with the angels."

"Jerry was at my mother's?"

"I have a witness. He may not have stayed long. But then, you don't need much time to squeeze a trigger."

"I told you," Carol said wearily. "I don't think Jerry's capable of any such thing."

"Then he'd better see a surgeon about that fork in his tongue."

"I can't help it if he lies," she snapped. She stopped short in the colorless hallway. "Lying's not the same as killing someone. And Jerry's not my worry anymore. Why should I go through all that garbage one more—"

"Because I'm beginning to hear bloodhounds."

"It's not my fault." She spit the words into my face. An old gent gaunt and fuzzy as a baby bluejay gawked at us from a wheelchair. Dr. C lowered her voice: "Let the bloodhounds chew his fanny off."

"Why would he want to kill your mother when—"

"Duncan, listen. I don't mean to take this out on you. And this isn't the right place."

"Have a bite with me after work."

"You make it sound like two dogs and a bone."

"Woof."

"How about Saturday afternoon? If the weather's good, we can play tennis on the roof court."

"Bark, bark."

"You do a lousy dog imitation."

I wagged my tail.

Chapter Sixteen

When I phoned Lieutenant Phil Auburn in Cambridge and asked what he knew about Jerry Schell's itinerary on the night of the murder, he was coy. "Tell me what you know."

"It's not much."

"I'll decide that."

"Thanks, Sahib."

"What?"

"Dorothy O'Hare's son-in-law was with her about the time she died. Drove her home in his fancy Jaguar."

"You talk to him?"

"First he lied, then he stonewalled."

The lieutenant couldn't resist a fatherly scolding: "You know, you guys make my job harder by putting him on his guard."

I passed up the obvious answer.

"The son-in-law quarrel with the victim?"

He made it sound like a chess game—knight quarreling with queen. I said, "My guess is they were competing for the woman's daughter from the first day. Dorothy O'Hare felt he wasn't good enough for her daughter."

"I thought you said he's a Back Bay lawyer."

"The guy wasn't always so golden. And unless I'm getting too old to read the social signs, he's gay. Whereas Dorothy O'Hare was an ambitious Hyde Park Catholic widow who'd worked her potatoes off to buy a house in Newton and make the daughter a glorious success. Jerry Schell may have threatened all that. She seems to have felt betrayed."

"But?"

"But Jerry Schell's just about divorced from the daughter. He's got a uranium-colored Jaguar. Why would he jeopardize everything for a ten-second thrill of revenge against his mother-in-law?"

"In my estimation queers tend to be devious about their anger. Bitchier. Besides which, I'm very old-fashioned. I believe in evil."

I made an all-purpose grunt. I believe in evil too, yet much of the time it makes a great soundtrack without explaining the story you see.

I gave Rachel the most recent satanic mail.

The next day she reported that the American Satan wasn't cutting up the Boston *Globe,* the *Herald American,* the *Monitor,* the *Times,* or the *New York Post.* She was going to try some alternative rags like the *Phoenix* and weak suburban papers like the *Middlesex News.*

It was Meg's day for surgery.

I went into Boston early, dropping Rachel at a stationery store to continue her research.

By lunchtime Meg was coming back from the land of nod. The nurses congratulated her on the outcome, then the plastic surgeon came in with his apprentices and congratulated himself. When traffic died down Meg said, "They try to match the color of the new eye to your real one."

"I'm always fooled."
She wasn't listening.
Rachel breezed in. She'd stopped into a hairdresser's and had her hair unspiked. It may have been a paler shade of green too. She downplayed my compliments—too proud to acknowledge the compromise she'd made. "How's the new eye?" she asked her mother.
They hugged. Daughter piled right into mother. Meg said, "I hear you're getting involved in your father's work."
"I've been checking in stationery stores. The hate mail seems to be put together with a glue stick, maybe a German one called Pritt. Comes in a tube like a stick deodorant."
"You're a genius," I said.
Her eyes blazed with purpose.

Pat Shaughnessy's eyes blazed with purpose too. I was rubbing noses with his married sister Eileen in her Charlestown living room when Shaughnessy came downstairs from his nap. It was a lived-in two-family house, its interior pasted over with squares of ceiling tile and bluish-gray driftwood paneling. On the shag rug her two sons were battling plastic space creatures back and forth. The flashy warriors were really old-fashioned tin soldiers without the sporting red uniforms and the tendency to line up for killing.
Shaughnessy was worried enough to postpone his rage. He plunged his fists deep into his green chino pockets and said huskily, "Didn't I warn you to keep off of me?"
He'd grown up in a house where a man's threat was supposed to silence opposition like the idea of an atom bomb. "Don't panic," I said. "Your sister's telling me about your complaint against Dr. Farhat."

"That scum."

Down on the rug one of the boys howled. "That's no fair! I got him. If he's dead, he has to stay dead!"

"Squelch it," Pat Shaughnessy called.

Perched on the plaid arm of the La-Z-Boy recliner, Eileen went on, "And these chiropractic birthday cards he would send, even. Anything to keep you coming back for the treatments. But really, it was the crooked billing got us. I mean, this guy billed Pat's insurance for seven visits he never even went to. You know how much money that is?"

"How does Dr. Farhat explain things?"

"He claims Pat never showed up for the appointments."

"But there never was no G-D appointments," Pat growled.

"That's right. There never was. I checked. I can read a damn calendar." She lowered her voice. "And that was a lot of money for us. At that point in time Pat'd gotten out of his insurance plan for, like, employment reasons."

Meaning he'd been under indictment for manslaughter.

"So," he put in, "them G-D visits added up fast. And I had lawyer bills and all this crap."

"And how did it resolve itself?"

"Once I told him I didn't have any insurance no more, he said we would split the bill. And when I said I didn't have that much, he said we'd do time payments. And when I said like hell, he said he'd finish the treatments and then I'd pay. And when I told him I didn't need treatments no more, he just shooed me off like a fly on dog shit. Then I could see that none of it meant anything to him. Even the money was, like, just a game to him. Even though it was going to squeeze me. So I almost put his teeth down his throat."

I switched on my anchorman voice: unfazed, factual, compassionate. I tried to include brother and sister alike in my steady gaze.

"Are you prepared to swear you haven't contacted Dr. Farhat in any manner or form in the last year?"

"Sure," Pat growled.

"I never heard Pat even mention him once."

"If it was necessary," I added, "would you be prepared to take a polygraph test to prove that?"

"Sure."

"Tomorrow?"

He was dogged: "Sure."

I stroked my chin, then took an Official Deep Breath: "As far as I'm concerned, unless new evidence warrants, you're no longer part of this investigation. Thanks for being so cooperative."

On the floor the kids were still warring. "Because why?"

"Because He-Man's killed Skeletor, see, and if you weren't so stupid you wouldn't keep moving him."

"You dummy."

"You're the total stupid nerd."

CHAPTER SEVENTEEN

From Carol's living room on Saturday you could see across Boston Harbor to Portugal. Shadows and noon sun tangled in the potted plants by the window. On the wall the African spirit mask was still flashing its hairy grin. Greetings from the honored ancestors. The glass-topped coffee table could have been a block of ice melting into the hot red Persian rug.

Carol was flustered. "You're early. I haven't even got the bed made yet."

"Let me help."

"I didn't invite you over here to make my bed."

"As you make your bed, so shall you lie in it."

"That sounds like a threat."

"I picture bed-making as a beach sport in a cola ad. Like volleyball."

"If it's sports you want, let's play tennis."

"I don't have a racket."

"Jerry's is here somewhere. I think it's clunky but he likes its firepower. He paid a fortune for it. I should give it to Morgan Memorial. Let some poor kid use it."

"Tennis isn't a poor kid's game. That's why I never really learned."

She fished a can of tennis balls out of the hall closet and handed me a racket. "Come on, sissy."

The rooftop court was breezy, sunny, and cool at the same time. You felt open to the sky, as if you could slam the ball across Scollay Square into Fenway Park. Yet you played inside a tall wire fence like lobsters in a trap. Across the water at Logan jets rose and descended, back and forth, over and over, like wasps servicing a nest.

We volleyed back and forth. In her white shorts and jersey Carol moved with slightly gawky elegance. She had a practiced backhand and a serve that could stop a rhino. Me, I trotted and swatted. What I needed was a lifestyle that naturally included some exercise. Once after a tedious product-counterfeiting case Vera and I rented bicycles for a week on Nantucket, and got sunburned watching them. In Chinese restaurants and in the lobbies of movie theaters we planned workouts and jogging routes, but that was as close as we got. On the other hand, we were still in shape enough to squeeze into the shower together.

Carol clobbered me. As we were calling it quits I said, "You put up a good fight."

She laughed: "When I realized you couldn't really play, I was going to go easy on you to be polite. Then I decided the hell with it, you're a big boy."

"You're a sweetheart."

"Bite a tennis ball." Her face was full of mischief. "If you don't play tennis, what do you do for fun?"

"I want to fly."

"You're not going to jump off the roof, are you?"

"Ever see an ultralight aircraft? Looks like a lawn mower with wings? I'm building one. A friend of ours will keep it on her farm in Connecticut. Just the ticket for a warm spring afternoon. You'd love it. Want to learn to fly?"

"I wouldn't trust myself. But maybe I'd change my mind if I watched you first." She flapped her arms, with the tennis rackets as wingtips, and made as if to take off over the harbor. The exercise had put color in her lovely face and a bouncy poise in her walk. Or maybe it was simply the first time I'd seen her happy.

Later, as we were clattering down the concrete staircase—the elevator wasn't working again—I said, "You're coming out of shock. I can feel it."

"Mmm. I don't think about Jerry. And as for my mother . . . well, in the hospital we see old ladies who are really hurting. Most of them would be grateful to make such a clean exit. So I tell myself it could've been worse."

"What does Jerry tell himself?"

She let us into the apartment. "I asked Jerry about driving my mother home that Thursday night. He was very open about it. As I told you, she'd bought a new car but it hadn't arrived yet." Carol filed the tennis rackets into the hall closet. "You want some tea?"

"Real tea or flower water?"

"You choose."

"Let's eat out then. On the way you can tell me what Jerry was doing with Dorothy and why he lied to me."

"Want to see if the saunas are open at this hour? All that steam can be heavenly after tearing around the tennis court."

"Sounds relaxing, but at the moment my stomach's bossing me around. You hungry?"

"I want to change first." Two steps into the room she balked: "But look, I'd rather spend an evening with you than an evening making excuses for Jerry."

"Good. But since you brought it up, did Jerry go into the house with your mother?"

She sighed: "For a second. To bring in some groceries."

"What did they fight about?"

"They didn't. Why should they fight? Jerry drove home. Maybe she should've locked the door then and didn't."

"So why is he rattled about admitting his visit?"

"Jerry's a little paranoid about the police."

"Because he's gay?"

Her eyebrows gave a rueful hop: "I guess he's not real subtle about that anymore, is he?"

"Or is it because he does drugs?"

Carol pursed her lips and blew off invisible steam: "I'd better put on some tea."

"Let's go out. We can talk while you're changing."

"Duncan, what's the use of all this?"

"I'll wait out in the hall."

While she dressed, I waited outside the bedroom door studying a framed photo she'd taken on a public health project two summers ago in Rwanda. A dusky black girl was directing a bull along a tricky hill path with a stick the size of a magic wand. Beside the little girl the bull looked huge and mild and dangerous. It was like a close-up of an ant pushing a live bullet up a hill.

"When you're a poor med student," Carol was saying, "when you're over your head in debt and hanging on for dear life, a lawyer who eats lunch with business big shots and owns a big sailboat, well, it makes a good impression."

"Jerry tried to tell me you were both starving when you got married."

"It turned out we were. My first big surprise."

"There were others."

"Hell, yes. He was always out late working on his briefs.

Peeling them off would be more like it. I used to think he was so sexy. And he must have been doing pills like the people he hung out with. As a med student"—blouse, bra, and skirt went sailing past the open door into a white hamper—"you run into uppers at exam times and Percodans or the like afterward. I won't say I never did any experimenting. But sometimes I think Jerry went out with me just because I could get my hands on pills. When he was high he was so caring. So into you. So completely unafraid. Nothing could hurt you."

"You loved the guy."

"It kills me to say it."

"Maybe he loved you too. Maybe it wasn't just brilliant acting."

"Nice thought. Good painkiller."

Out over the harbor the reddish sky had drained toward blues and ocean gray. A navy destroyer sat in the channel off South Boston making smoke but no wake. Along Atlantic Avenue a police car was blinking in mute emergency. In the glass skyline lights were coming on. As we headed for the elevator Carol said suddenly, "See what a baby I was? All I'd ever done was work, work, work."

"I've seen worse traits in a kid."

"No, really. All I knew how to do was reach. Just a grabby little robot. I can't even blame my mother, since she survived after my father died by turning into a grabby robot herself."

"What's your idea of a grabby robot? Give me an example."

"Oh I don't blame her. I owe her who I am. But I have to be realistic too. Since my mother died I've started to feel I know hardly anything about me."

"You're not completely in the world until you lose both your parents. At least that's how it hit me."

"I think I married Jerry to postpone that day."
"When did your father die?"
"At Easter. In third grade." She hesitated: "Suicide."
"Ouch."
"Mmm. I used to think I just outlived it somehow. Now I'm not so sure." She sucked in a breath: "I think I began feeling everything through rubber gloves."
"Like a doctor."
"It turns you off, me being a doctor."
"Sometimes."
"Make you feel competitive?"
"Not just that."
"Better if I was just a cute homebody?"
"Hell no."
"What then?"
"Antiseptic breath."
"Are you joking?"
"Most doctors I know, they're always a little bit on guard. Never quite at home in the world. They see the germs on everything."
"Like investigators."
I grinned: "But they tend to be very sharp people. And that wins me over."
The elevator opened into the cavernous garage. I put my arm on Carol's shoulder and—something about the ease of our bodies—I sensed pleasure in the gloomy air.
"We'll take my car," Carol said. "Where do we eat?"
"How about the Four-Loaf Cleaver?"
"You can't afford it."
"How can you tell?"
"Come on, Duncan. I don't smell money on you. Here's the key. You drive."
We shot out of the underground garage in the BMW.
"As you get older," I said, "your life gets stranger."

"How about strange food? There's a terrific Ethiopian restaurant on Tremont Street. The Addis. Or wait. There's a take-out place in Dorchester. They're Thai, the food's really tasty. And a nosy New Yorker and his boring girlfriend can afford it."

"Girlfriend?"

She was flustered: "Hospital people are always kidding around. Haven't you noticed?"

We sprinted down the Southeast Expressway, then cut into the old city of cheek-to-cheek triple-deckers, toward Fields Corner. The Great Star Restaurant occupied a Depression-era storefront with a fancy tin ceiling and an expired soda fountain that played a bar. Black and white mosaic in the floor by the door spelled out bygone occupants, the Palermo Social Club. Cello-wrapped chopsticks on the Formica tables now, and stacks of take-out containers behind the cash register. It was a family venture: everybody behind the counter working the woks and chopping blocks with single-minded ferocity. They were new immigrants, still trying to throw a saddle on the English language. You couldn't help rooting for them.

Every day in my business I saw what the gurus were calling the deindustrialization of America. Factories turning into condos for Jerry Schells to sink their paper profits into. All the action was in real-estate speculation and leveraged buy-outs of other people's leveraged buy-outs. It felt good to see the crew of the Great Star Restaurant actually making something.

They knew how to cook. And we knew how to eat: spicy crabs and chicken-with-cashews. Instead of flower tea, we drank Thai beer with a mild ricey flavor. I asked, "How much of an estate has your mother left?"

"Do you have to be on the job every minute? Can't you just enjoy yourself?"

"The pleasure's in getting to know you."

"Me or my checkbook?"

"Are you a rich heiress now?"

"Fat chance. Dorothy didn't leave much, apart from the house. That's worth something of course, given these crazy Boston prices. But we had to remortgage it to pay for school."

"Got any other med-school loans?"

"Who doesn't?"

"How much?"

"If I don't tell you, will you snoop around till you find out?"

"Shall I tell you what I make a year?"

"First you, then me? Like skinny-dipping? You strip, then I have to?"

"We can try skinny-dipping too if you want. But first things first."

"I might have to sell the house in Newton. Do you have any idea what it costs to go into private practice now?"

"Planning to open an office?"

"Mmm. But everything interests me. First I might try working with the Fertility Clinic at the hospital. Or the AIDS research group."

"Because of Jerry?"

"In a way." She twiddled a crableg with her chopsticks. "Actually that's how it came to an end. The marriage, I mean." She nibbled the hot crabmeat. "I found out that Jerry'd had himself tested for the AIDS virus. For two weeks I was sick to my stomach. All the little details fell into place. I'd known but I hadn't let myself know. He had another life out there, and for all I knew he'd infected me too. I've never been so scared. Scared and humiliated. To be killed so stupidly, by someone you've— God Almighty—"

"That explains a lot."

She watched me with big, wide-open eyes. "Why I'm so frozen up, you mean."

"Not what I said."

"Liar," she said sweetly. "I shouldn't have panicked, but when you're working in a hospital it's easy to get spooked." She swigged her beer. "What killed me was realizing how driven I'd been. I mean, here I'd married this hunk of a guy thinking I knew him inside out, like your teddy bear from baby days. I had it all figured out, the house we'd live in, the plants on the kitchen windowsill—I could tell you the names of our three kids. The whole daydream."

"Everybody's living in some kind of dream future."

"Well mine was insane."

"It hurt your pride."

"It scared me to death. What killed me was realizing how asleep I'd been—the whole time, *not there*. Sometimes I think, what if I'm still blind, even at work, following all the rules, and I'm letting someone die?"

"The day I met you, you seemed so sure of yourself. Even bossy. The typical doctor."

"I love my work."

"It scares you too."

"Nobody wants to live a frozen-up life."

"Maybe you need a change."

"I love the work, but when you can't keep on top of things, say you lose a patient, you see it coming, you're helpless to stop it, you feel, well. . ."

"Dead."

"And guilty. See, you know perfectly well what I'm talking about." She stared at the dismembered crab on her plate, triumphant and miserable. "So what do you do about it?"

"Learn what you can." I shrugged. "Love what you can."

"I've been on ice since I left Jerry."

"By choice?"

She shook her head: "I haven't been feeling very desirable since I've been on my own again."

"You want me to tell you how desirable you are?"

"Sure."

"Okay. Mucho."

"Heavens! I'm turning into a pumpkin."

I liked flirting with her: not with the slightly stilted idealist but with the startled sleepwalker who was waking up as a woman with big responsibilities. A softness came into her eyes and the corners of her mouth that set my heart drumming. "You want that desirable crableg?" I asked.

She shook her head: "Try it."

It was delicious. I said, "With radioactive raindrops coming down and killer viruses wearing designer undies, it's not an easy world for lovers."

"If you're a woman doctor, you're always meeting men who want you to take care of them."

"How about other docs?"

"They're too busy keeping you in your place."

"Ah."

"What I love is hanging out with a guy who's just a guy."

"Such as?"

She shrugged, studying my knuckles. I felt something stirring in my wok. I covered her hand.

"How'd you make peace with Jerry?"

Her eyes darkened: "You mean, did he have the disease? Am I safe to fuck?"

"Don't be so touchy."

"We were lucky. Jerry claimed he'd fooled around only once. With a guy who was sick now. An old college pal, a track-team partner. Supposedly Jerry gave in only because the guy was so lonely—an errand of mercy. It was the silliest story you ever heard. Which just made it worse for me. I screamed at him. I had fantasies about pushing him out the roof window in that funny little bathroom we had on Melrose Street. And yet I knew he couldn't help himself. He seemed so helpless, so ignorant. I just wanted to get away."

"You loved him."

"Or maybe med school rots your mind."

"I know just the cure."

"Tell me what's good for me."

We spent the evening on Carol's sofa prescribing goodness for each other. Across the harbor East Boston was lit up like the roller coaster at Nantasket way back when. Planes knifed in and out of Logan, one step ahead of the roar they left behind. With the room lights down the African mask on the wall hovered in space like a ghostly ancestor.

The woman in my arms wanted to tell me about her months in Rawnda, with a memory so vivid that I broke into a sweat hearing about the humid African afternoons and slapped at the bedtime mosquitoes. The beauties of the landscape knocked my eye out. The trip had been Carol's first escape from the ghetto of suburban achievement she'd grown up in. Her first taste of life really. She'd had a public-health fellowship, and loved those months. Loved the people, the kids. I took it all in. You never know when you'll need a little background in natural childbirth, waterborne parasites, and African VD.

We sampled some Nigerian juju music—Yoruba vocals, guitars, and talking drums: strong, subtle rhythms your body breathes in. The two of us swayed on the yielding rug, barefoot. Carol let the rhythms pick her up and shake her like a skirt on a clothesline in a rippling spring breeze. I said, "You must like jazz."

"Uh-uh. It doesn't have any melody."

"But you like this."

"African music is different from everything. That's what I meant before. When you're there you feel you really matter. And it's beautiful because it doesn't matter that you're heroic. You don't get twisted over it. You're just doing what you have to do and some people are feeling better because of it. I'd like to go back there for a few years."

Somehow fiddling with her bra I missed her reasoning. She snuggled against me: "You smell good." She was discouraging my search for a zipper in the seams of her skirt. "I like breathing you in," she apologized. "But it takes a while, getting personal."

"You're right, that's half the fun." On its way to the armchair, the bra caught on the lampshade and dangled. She pressed into me, arms tight around my chest:

"That's not what I mean."

"Tell me what you mean."

"If I, you know, if we just screw around, it's nothing. It's— I'm not saying this right."

I kissed her ear: "As my Vermont granny used to say, don't peel the apple if you're not hungry."

"I know, I feel like a dumb kid."

"Why don't I just touch your nipples real timidly while we discuss African parasites."

"Don't make fun of me. I mean, I like it when . . ."

Her ear tasted salty.

"Med school was so tense, like a war or something, and I went to bed with everybody, even the ones I didn't like, that looked down on you—especially them. I was like some kind of rapist: we'd be studying endocrinology, and all of a sudden, uh-oh, look out. Or even in the basement of the damn library—what an idiot."

She began telling me about prep school and dances and the embarrassment of being a poor nobody trying to dress up like money. It was scornful and self-involved, this monologue, but also funny. She was smart about herself, and I enjoyed her, tickling and then scratching her back. Dreamily, furiously, she said, "My childhood was nothing but this, this *report* card. I'll tell you, I went into medicine because I was dying of boredom."

"Don't give up."

My hands studied the curves and living muscle of the female gluteus maximus.

"Hey," she whispered. "Really. I'm chicken."

"So be it. But you're also one of the most grown-up people I know. You have a beautiful soul, deep insights, and a very creamy crotch at the moment."

"God, you really lay it on pretty thick, don't you."

"Offended?"

"Let me rub against your skin some more to get warm."

Chapter Eighteen

Dr. Farhat pestered me for advice. How do you detect a car bomb? Should he make it a point never to leave his house or office by the same door he entered? Should he have the bushes by the house cut back so no one could hide there?

But Mehdi's activities were hardly coming to a halt. The *Sunday Globe*'s real-estate section included an architectural sketch of a health complex to be built in Norwood by Sunrise Associates. In addition to practitioners' offices, the plan called for a fitness center, tennis club, and a range of health-food and sporting-goods stores. The chrome-and-glass extravaganza was to be called "Wellness Plaza," a project of Dr. Mehdi Farhat, the "well-known health advocate who arrived from Iran more than a decade ago owning nothing but a plastic raincoat." Now among his grateful admirers he counted the Duchess of Windsor, who had urged him to "spread the word."

When I mentioned the article, Mehdi slapped his leather-topped desk and wailed: "It was months ago I talked to those newspaper people. I forgot. Who needs this publicity? 'The Iranian immigrant.' Exactly I don't want to be that now."

Tuesday at the hospital Carol took me down to the cafeteria on her break. Since the weekend we seemed inclined to bump or rub each other going through doors. We sat knee-to-knee at a corner table sticky with coffee stains while I ate a tunafish who'd died between spongy squares of whitebread. Carol folded the plastic wrap into a small crinkled diamond.

"I think I'm being followed."

"You invited me here."

"No, really. Last night I drove over to see my Aunt Gladys in Hyde Park, and the same headlights stayed behind me the whole way. Even when I deliberately zigzagged out of my way. Was that you?"

I shook my head: "What kind of car?"

"It was too dark. When I pulled over to watch him pass, he stopped behind me. The whole time I had a prickly sensation on the back of my neck, like a gun was aimed there. I had this horrible sense they could drive up, shoot me to death in my car, and drive off into the night, and it would be in the papers one day and that would be the end of it. That really, anybody can kill anybody. Dog eat dog. I . . . Jesus, I got the creeps. I'll tell you, I floored the gas pedal and I didn't let up till I was in Glady's living room. God, I wish you'd been with me."

"Shall I tag along on your way home tonight?"

"I hate to drag you around like that. What if I'm just imagining things?"

"I can't help feeling protective toward you."

"Maybe I was spooked because I'd gotten a panicky call from Jerry. As you predicted, the state police have been questioning him. A Lieutenant Andrews or Anderson."

"Auburn."

"Jerry's afraid the guy has a bug about gays. He's afraid they'll fake evidence against him. After all, Jerry's fingerprints are on the back door, and Mrs. Day says she saw him there Thursday evening."

"You can't hang a guy for helping his mother-in-law with the groceries."

"A scandal would damage his practice."

"Did one of them owe the other money, by any chance?"

"Not likely."

"He do any work for her?"

"Jerry mostly works on estates and corporation stuff. Besides, what did my mother ever own that required a lawyer?"

"For a churchmouse," I said, "your mother managed to starve in style."

"Dorothy was pretty careful with a buck."

"Do you mind if I have a look through her house?"

"I thought you already had."

"That was at night."

"Well, I have to sort through her things in a couple days. Come with me. What do you think you'll find?"

I gave an all-purpose shrug: "Not many lady bookkeepers can keep a big house in Newton and dip down to Aruba in February."

"Dr. Farhat always gave her a big holiday bonus. She ran everything for him, even some of his real-estate investments. He's a clever investor."

"The *Globe* thinks so."

"You saw that piece?" She seemed pleased.

"I thought M.D.s were supposed to be very suspicious of chiropractors."

"Oh the chiropractic theory is silly. But sometimes

people are rotten with anxiety and the laying on of hands may help. Or just as massage it may work. I used to get neck spasms worse than the electric chair, and Mehdi got me out of it."

"What makes Mehdi such a clever investor?"

"He's very intuitive. He senses inner energies and potentials."

"I don't mean his juju. I mean, what has he invested in?"

"Real estate. Stocks too, I think. Why?"

"I wonder if he owes any of his success to your mother."

"He went to the track with her once or twice. Mother had a great head for numbers. You'd play cards with her and she'd know from the discards what was in your hand. When she bet at Foxboro she could weigh all the facts about each horse in her head at once. So she never lost much."

"They were pals."

"Dr. Farhat kept us afloat sometimes when we were just about finished." She grinned at her own melodrama. "No, seriously. That's how it was, living with my mother. Always drowning and saved from drowning. That's just how it felt. When I was a little kid, she'd get fired and come home and say, 'Start putting your dolls in boxes, say good-bye to your friends, we have to move.' And just as I'd get myself all worked up for moving day, after crying myself to sleep for a week, she'd get us rescued. One time she—"

The beeper at her waist went off. The big-eyed dreamy woman suddenly turned into the militant Dr. C: "Sorry. Got to go." She was half out of her seat when she added: "I'm sorry about the other night. I wanted to but I couldn't. Kind of childish, I know."

"You can make it up to me."

"I've been thinking about you, making a space for you." She ducked her eyes: "I'll be thinking about you all afternoon."

"Me too. Let's rub two thoughts together and make a fire. Pick an evening."

"Call me?"

"Sooner than that."

"You're pushing."

"You're worth it."

She made an undignified noise at me that some of our fellow diners found pretty intriguing.

Chapter Nineteen

Meg's house in Natick is a typical New England saltbox. It's gotten neater and frillier since I lived there. As I was mixing up hot salsa burritos for supper, Rachel yelled down from upstairs: "Sean's on the phone. Okay if we go to the Wellesley College library to study tonight?"

Wellesley College is just over the town line, on the far side of snobbery, but it also offered a little romantic privacy. Rachel felt me hesitate.

"I can check out more newspaper typefaces for you. And I want to look at some college catalogs."

Playing expertly on the old man's heartstrings.

After supper I put on the coffeepot and skimmed through the day's mail, including a white post-office envelope addressed to me. I unzipped it with one tine of my fork. Even before my eyes registered it, I felt the wrinkly patches of paper paste:

> LAST warning
> Back OFF
> or goodBY GirL

There was no signature, but the format was unmistakable. Nobody had my Natick address, not even Mehdi Farhat.

So somebody was following me. I phoned Mehdi to see if he'd received a note too. But today I had the devil all to myself. Now I began to worry about the goodBY GirL, so I tried Carol.

"God," she exhaled, "you think it means me?"

"All the evidence of my senses tells me you are a girl."

"Are you going to do as he says? You know, back off?"

"I'll have to sleep on it."

"It's getting too dangerous to know you."

"Is that a joke?"

"If I were you, I'd drop this whole business."

I heard the unspoken worry: *You'll get me killed.*

"Pretty soon," I said, "it starts costing me money."

"Every time I go out now I'll feel eyes watching me."

I went over some precautions with Carol and hung up wondering if I had misjudged Don Frazier or Shaughnessy. Or was this Jerry Schell's ploy to deflect attention away from him? Or a threat coming from an unforeseen angle?

GoodBY GirL.

And where is your daughter tonight, Mr. Ames?

By nine-thirty I was talking myself into a personal reconnaissance of the Wellesley College library when Sean's car pulled up and Rachel waltzed in triumphantly.

"Guess where your Satan got his cut-out newspaper words."

"I give up."

"No really. Guess. You'll never get it."

"The *Bombay Times*."

"Uh-uh. *The Wall Street Journal*. How's that for a fake-me-out? I was getting ready to give up on the whole project. And then, pow! There it was. I could hardly believe my eyes. But that's it. The typefaces match up perfectly."

As you'd expect, Lieutenant Auburn took a deep interest in the typography of *The Wall Street Journal*. Over the phone his voice gave a short sniffing laugh: "I bet I know someone who's a regular subscriber to *The Wall Street Journal*."

"His ex-wife, the doctor, tells me Schell had no grudge against her mother. So what have we got for a motive?"

"For one thing, it looks like Mr. Schell's got a sick sex life going."

Phil Auburn assumed that only freaks commit crimes. I asked, "And what did you say the motive was?"

"This is all preliminary, Ames. Just scouting the territory. Let me know what else you uncover."

"What do you think about the threats against my daughter?"

"If this is a Satan who reads the financial pages, I'd say nobody's in any danger."

"On the other hand, Dorothy O'Hare is dead. And it's possible Jerry Schell didn't send those notes."

"In that case I'd say you got a problem."

▽

Chapter Twenty

On Friday afternoon, every room of Dorothy O'Hare's house felt cold. The cold clung to things like a thin layer of grease. The ravine out back blocked the May sunshine that rollicked through the rest of the neighborhood.

Perhaps because of the chill the fancy living room didn't invite you to sit and put up your feet. In the magazine rack, harness-racing forms mixed with *House Beautiful*. The saltshaker had the dining-room table all to itself. Digging for bullets the cops had gouged a whitish hole among the dark-red poppies on the wallpaper. The rug was gone. "I had the cleaning people haul it away," Carol said. "For obvious reasons."

She hit the thermostat and pushed on to the kitchen. I heard her begin emptying the refrigerator. The oil burner grumbled in the cellar.

"Where did Dorothy keep her papers and bills?"

"I cleaned out her desk. The stuff's in a cardboard box up in her bedroom."

"I'll have a look."

Dorothy's bedroom was high enough to catch the last sun skimming over the hill. On the path that snaked down from the school, kids were playing cops and robbers. The radiator began to hiss in the corner. A white tufted spread covered the high twin bed, and the Governor Winthrop desk was made of real cherry. A cardboard carton held an assortment of records: bank statements, insurance forms, an invoice for the new Mercedes that Dorothy had never picked up.

I sorted through the papers trying to read the desires and fears they implied. There was a newspaper clipping about the burning of Mehdi Farhat's nursing home, including an obit for the fireman who'd died. Other tidbits included old plumbers' bills, mortgage receipts, a rebate coupon for smoke detectors, and an upbeat ad in which Dr. Farhat explained how he could manipulate the plates of your child's skull to relieve mental retardation.

"Fridge's empty," Carol said. "Some of that stuff was just about to go stinko." Out of her medical whites, wearing fresh jeans with her hair pulled back, she had a girl-next-door bounciness that made me smile. She squeezed down beside me on the bed: "What'd you find?"

"Not much so far. Have you seen your mother's checkbook?"

"I took it to give the lawyer. The will has to be probated or whatever they do."

"Any unusual outlays in the checkbook?"

"I never looked."

"Not once?"

"I'm not a snoop."

She fell into me, fooling around. My arm corralled her and I let myself lean toward the pillow. She leaned away. She pointed to the treadle sewing machine in the corner, an old Singer trimmed in filigree gilt. "See that? My mother won a department-store Easter Parade contest with a dress she sewed on that machine."

"I thought you won the contest."

"It was her dress."

"You were a beautiful kid."

"Sometimes she'd get inspired and stay up all night. As a kid I used to think everybody's mother stayed up all night doing fantastic projects like fairy-tale elves. I'd wake up to pee and you'd hear that sewing machine clattering away like monkeys rattling their cages. Next morning she'd drag out of bed and go to work as if nothing'd happened."

I stretched out: "Come let me out of my cage."

She sat up on the edge of the bed: "She didn't even *like* to sew. But if she wanted something, she had to do it herself."

"Good for her."

"One morning when I went downstairs Dorothy was stripping wallpaper. The easy places first, in big patches. For months we had big ragged holes all over, like a war. She laid a guilt trip on me for not finishing the job for her. I was in fifth grade then. She used to say, 'Life's too short for dreams.' "

Carol sat bolt upright on the edge of the bed. My fingers did a soothing chiropractic number on her back.

"I've got an ache," she said. "Right by the shoulder blade."

I hiked her blouse and undid this and that. She had wonderful skin. I teased up goose bumps and then massaged till she pushed to her feet.

"Come in my room. It's warmer."

I tugged at her waistband. She pulled away.

"No, really, I can't relax in here."

She pulled her blouse together and went across the hall. As I started to get up I felt something edgy under the pillow. A pocket diary. A pocket diary with appointments, phone numbers, birthdays to remember, and a final notation: "Close Dedham Forty. Title. Esc. Seller pays termite." There on May 28, still a couple weeks away, Dorothy's calendar went blank.

I love a good puzzle.

"Hey," Carol called, "you mad at me?"

"I'm rattling my cage."

"Chimp want peanuts?"

I tossed the question back at her with a pun. She grinned.

For some reason it gave me a twinge, the sight of her there in her old bed with the quilt pulled up to her nose. Trying on childhood again, I suppose. The teddy bear still slouched on the nightstand with his nose bandaged in a handkerchief—always the doctor. The skeleton on the bookshelf was still envying the gaudy ceramic birds on the dresser. The crocheted snowflake dangled from the ceiling light. Carol watched me taking it in. I knew by the rise and fall of the blanket on the tips of her breasts what I would find underneath.

Set those monkeys free.

We rolled around a bit getting warm, appreciating each other. We'd slipped each other's shirts off when Carol murmured, "You grunt so sweetly."

"Ummm."

"You're older than me."

"Don't rub it in."

She checked out the hairs on my chest for gray. The cool quilt kept her nipples at attention. I said, "I love it when you give me that sneaky grin."

"Oh?"

"I like to see you happy."

"Is that all?"

"And you have a cute ass for a doctor."

She fought back. "I admire you too. You have a— Did you bring a condom?"

"A condom?" I laughed: "I don't even carry a pistol."

"I didn't think either."

"You have a diaphragm."

"How did you—?" She was offended. "Well, it doesn't matter. I don't sleep with strangers. It's too dangerous."

"You're safe with me."

"That's what they all say."

"I've been George Washington with you."

"That's what they all say. You're an investigator, for God's sakes." She was smiling and not smiling. "You meet too many women."

"The only woman I've slept with— What the hell, I don't have to report to you."

"Only if we're going to be lovers. What's your partner's name? Laura?"

"Vera. Don't jump to conclusions." I put some hot breath on one cold nipple. And a warm tongue.

"Wait."

I didn't. She insisted. I insisted. She gave me a strategic squeeze that hurt. I stopped insisting. She took her hand away.

"Wait," she murmured. "Please." She touched her lips to my knuckles. "I can't. Not without some precaution. I trust you. But not completely."

"Then you don't trust me."

"Look, Duncan. Be serious. With this virus, if you guess wrong you die." She gave my cheek a motherly pat. "I can't help being a damn doctor."

"And I can't help my trade either."

"That's why God gave us rubber, lover."

"You think because I work as a—"

"I think you're a sort of doctor. Trying to understand sickness in people just as I do." She chucked my chin with her knuckles: "And you don't give up either."

"Does the abbreviation 'Close Dedham forty' mean anything to you?"

"Uh-uh."

"Does this mean anything to you?"

I touched my lips to hers, once, very lightly, and drew back. She held her breath for a moment, then: "What next?"

"It's up to you. Whatever you feel."

"God, a man who wants to know what I feel. That's a new twist." Her eyes grew moist. "Guys don't usually ask me that."

"What's the answer?"

She ducked her eyes: "I feel like such a doctor, wanting to be in charge with you."

"Want me to be sick?"

A grin came over her: "Doctors aren't just obsessed with diseases, you know."

"Is that so?"

"Bodies ought to be a tremendous source of pleasure. I mean, why shouldn't a doctor be an expert about what feels good?"

"Is there a doctor in the house?"

Her grin widened: "Just me."

"You're all I need."

"I'm very confused about you," she whispered. Under the covers she was taking me in hand, with tenderness that melted even my hard heart.

Chapter Twenty-One

When we got back to the hospital Meg had her bed cranked up for supper. Every day her face had more color, less bandage. She was losing weight in the hospital, looking like her leaner and younger self. The new eye was a fine fake, though she tended to keep her eyes closed out of shyness. Tonight she puckered up for my kiss instead of turning her other cheek.

When I showed Meg the cryptic list in Dorothy's pocket diary, she waved it away. "Looks like a real-estate transaction."

"That's what I was thinking."

"A forty-acre property out in Dedham. 'Title' could be title search. 'Esc.' might be escrow. And the seller pays for the termite inspection."

"But what kind of property could a poor bookkeeper buy out in the suburbs?"

"Dog house maybe."

"I'll have Rachel check it out."

"That's no business for a girl her age. She barely touches her schoolwork as it is."

"She needs things to do that matter."

"If she's bored, she should put in the plants we ordered."

"She says you ordered them."

"Rachel hates gardens. Just like you do."

"Who says I hate gardens?"

"Then you plant the stuff."

"I'll fix the lawn mower before I go. That's my Boy Scout deed for the month."

"You think it's women's work to get down in the dirt."

"And what's men's work?"

"Spending sixteen hours a day sneaking up on people to find out their dirty faults."

"You're doing a pretty good job of exposing my dirty faults."

"Sorry. When you lie here cooped up in these damn casts and everything hurts . . . I mean, after too many days you—it's nobody's fault—you just, you want to lash out."

The way she crinkled her eyes shut I could feel her frustration. I put my open palm on her stomach: "Very tense. Tsk-tsk, even twitching."

I began to knead her gut. We used to joke about this as making pizza. Meg sighed: "Your client Dr. Farhat was by this afternoon. He's going to help get me loosened up when I've healed a bit more. He massaged my back. It took some of the tension out of me, it felt good. We had a really good talk. I felt like I've known him for years."

"He's cozy," I said kneading pizza.

"Don't spoil it." She winced, suddenly close to tears. "God, my muscles are frozen."

"You'll thaw."

Rachel had gone out for ice cream with her friend Sean, so the house was lonesome. I phoned Vera in New York.

"Duncan!" she gasped. "So you're not dead. I was just

scraping your name off the office door. I'd better pull your gear off the sidewalk before the dustmen cart it away."

"I've meant to call."

"Oh stuff it. What's the matter with you? Has Meg taken a bad turn?"

"Meg's fine, it's—"

"Are you in love?"

"My murder's growing on me."

"We pay the office rent on the fifteenth of the month."

"My satanic pen pal has begun threatening me, so I must be doing something right. If nothing develops in another week, I'll be back in New York."

"How's Rachel?"

"She's the one who discovered that our so-called American Satan has been making his notes out of snippets of *The Wall Street Journal*."

"Well that's cute."

"You see how teasingly things tie together?"

"Frankly, no."

"The murdered woman's son-in-law is a lawyer. I've seen the *Journal* in his office."

"That's fascinating. And this long-distance palaver means a big phone bill."

"You have a way with words, Vee."

"Why don't you dash down this weekend to catch me up on the plot?"

"Maybe Sunday night. If I can."

"I'm starting to get moody about men's underwear ads."

"That's sobering. I'll be back straightaway, love."

"And stop making fun of my accent."

"Straightaway."

After we hung up I watched the eleven-o'clock weatherman and wondered where the devil Rachel was. Which is when the doorbell finally rang. I went to the front hall to let her in. "Hey kid" or some such greeting was on my tongue when I started to pull the door inward. But as the words left my tongue, the storm-door glass shattered and the wood below the mail slot splintered with a dirty noise.

Son of a bitch.

My face was already down on the hall rug by the time my brain concluded it was a gunshot. I made a mental note to pick up some defensive hardware if I got to Manhattan on the weekend. Then I began crawling to the phone. Out front a car tore off in a blurry racket.

The presence of cops encourages you to walk upright. They helped me marvel at the splintery bullet hole in the front door, but that was about all they could do. The hole was too low to have killed a standing adult. I thought of the Red Brigade's tactic of kneecapping.

Ineptitude or intimidation. Take your pick.

The visitor had unscrewed the outside lightbulb, punched the doorbell, then made it back to his waiting car before the house door opened. A one-shot good-bye.

"I'm involved in a business investigation," I told the cops.

"Somebody's sending you a message."

"So I notice."

"Get a look at the car?"

"I was too busy eating lint off the rug."

He nodded: "We'll send a cruiser by here a couple times tonight."

"That leaves a few unguarded moments."

"Let me put it to you this way. With this Proposition 2½ on the taxes we're lucky to keep a guy on the switchboard. Call in if you notice any suspicious vehicles on the street."

"How long does it take to process a gun permit in Massachusetts?"

We were still discussing regulations when Rachel and Sean drove up. "Sorry we're late," Rachel chirped preemptively. "What's going on?"

Sean fingered the bullet hole, then went outside and lined up the entry hole with the one the slug made in the closet door behind it. "Fired from a car all right," he called. For him it was like TV only there was an actual hole in the door.

After Sean went home Rachel headed for the kitchen to scoop the peanut-butter jar onto a saltine. I poured a Hopfenperl beer: "Where the hell were you guys so late?"

"We stopped by the high school for a sec to help with the senior-play sets, and this little thing needed work, and that little thing was dumb, and blah blah blah."

For some reason Rachel's shorthand "Blah blah blah" bugged me. "Who said you could go up to the high school?"

"I'm not a baby."

"I expected you back. You should've phoned."

"Somebody's stuffed Kleenex in the cafeteria pay phone."

"That's not good enough. I need to know."

"Wow, what a tyrant."

"Grow up, kid. Some wise guy out there's popping away at your front door, and you—"

"Oh Dad, you're just flustered because of this—this *incident*. It's not going to happen again, is it?"

"I don't know."

"Well what do we do about it?"

"For starters, we don't go places on impulse and stay late."

"Oh brother! I can't just crawl under my bed and rot because you've got some weirdo mad at you."

"We can spend part of the weekend in Manhattan for a change of scene."

"New York?" she wailed. "I told Sean I'd be around."

"Can't be helped. I have to go into the city, and you can't stay here alone. In fact I don't want you to go anywhere alone for a while. I care about you, kid."

"Oh right!" She was furious. The adrenaline seemed to let down suddenly in angry tears: "Why did you have to come back here and ruin everything!"

CHAPTER TWENTY-TWO

IN THE MORNING I phoned Mehdi Farhat: "Someone assassinated my door last night." I sketched in the action.

"This is very terrible," Mehdi groaned. "I'm going to hire a security man to watch my house." He hesitated: "I hope you're not offended, Duncan. The man will hardly be the security genius you are. But I can't expect you to stand on guard around my pine trees all night."

"Speaking of houses. Ever considered buying real estate in Dedham?"

"My resources are invested in my medical complex, Spirit Plaza in Norwood. We were calling it Wellness Plaza, but don't you think Spirit sounds more positive? This will be a big, big—"

"We've talked about that."

"Oh." He was disappointed: he had his wings spread for takeoff.

"Dorothy O'Hare ever mention investing in real estate?"

He sighed: "Not very likely. Her own house was too much headache for one woman. She wanted to retire in peace."

"One more dead end. If you need me again, leave a message at my New York number."

"I'm sorry you must go to a new case."

We wept together.

After greasing out on a honeydip donut I sought out Dorothy O'Hare's friendly full-service bank in Newton Corner. The gal at the loan desk was the amiable Judy Kerouac, fortyish and almost blond, with a wide pixie mouth that smiled and then, when she mistook me for Dorothy O'Hare's executor, just as vividly mourned. "Oh yes," she said flipping through her file, "the loan was approved. One-fifty-five Oakdale Terrace in Dedham. Two-family house. Forty thousand dollars. Mr. Hackner checked it out for the bank and thought it was significantly underpriced. In need of a fix-up but basically just fine."

"Why such a remarkable bargain?"

"Lucky maybe." Ms. K gave an emphatic pixie-ish shrug. "The house is part of an estate."

"Who's the realtor?"

"There doesn't appear to be one."

"Odd."

"Maybe Mrs. O'Hare had connections to the family." The light in Judy Kerouac's eye told you this pixie was no fool.

"Who's the lawyer liquidating the estate?"

"Somebody in— Here it is. Barnet, Moser, and Schell. Marlboro Street, in Boston."

"I know the firm."

"They can answer all your questions, I'm sure."

"Thanks."

But don't count on it.

I tracked down Carol on her rounds at the hospital. She was with an assortment of doc types, all sizes and shapes.

In this hospital corridor of mud-brown lockers, clipboard crooked in her arm, she could have been a high-school girlfriend.

"Duncan," she said, startled. "Is everything all right?"

"Uh-uh." I watched her eyes widen. She came out of the group so I could add, "I need your mother's checkbook."

"Why?"

"Has she made any payments to realtors or lawyers?"

"We've been over this before."

"Well?"

"Well what? I don't know of any. Half the time my mother didn't have a nickel. What would she be doing with realtors? Look, I can't keep everybody here waiting."

"You have her checkbook. At home?"

"Yes but—"

"Let me have the key."

"Don't be so pushy," she grumbled.

"If your mother spotted a bargain property and put some money on her hunch, you stand to make a killing on it."

"Who cares," she muttered. "Listen. I lost a patient last night. A woman I liked. So I'm feeling shaky at the moment. And I've got to go."

Carol didn't move. In a way her doctor duds constrained her as much as any straitjacket. I said: "What say we run over to the apartment for lunch?"

"You're sweet," she said neutrally.

Touchy, touchy.

At noon Carol was still brittle. While I scanned her mother's check register she slapped together sandwiches: boysenberry jam from a California monastery and fresh-ground peanut butter free of additives and gritty as sawdust. She perched on a tall stool in the kitchenette.

"When you lose a patient like we did last night, you worry that Pathology will find some catastrophic little detail you overlooked. Some mistake. It's not like screwing up your knitting and ripping the stitches out to fix it."

I went around behind her chair. My arm looped down across her chest, around her waist, and my cheek pressed against the nape of her neck. "You'll be okay," I murmured. "Don't lose your nerve."

"Say that again. I just need to let this stuff blow. Just once. In fact I feel better. Thanks. Sorry for barking at you this morning. Sometimes I don't think."

While we choked down the gourmet peanut butter, I searched through Dorothy O'Hare's check register for the meaning of life, wondering out loud, "How could a real-estate investment not leave any paper traces?"

"So what's the big deal about my mother?"

"Dorothy made a brilliant stab in the real-estate market. Either she was some kind of investment psychic or she had help from some terrific elves."

"Jerry?"

"I suppose he hears about real-estate closings, estate settlements and the like?"

"My mother was always pestering him for inside tips. You know, trying to grab something before it came on the market and got bid way up."

"Well, she did it. The question is, will the cops find a motive for murder in it."

"That's ridiculous. Anybody can buy property."

"Maybe your mother forced sensitive information out of Jerry."

"Forced? How?"

I shrugged: "She knew about his awkward private life."

"That would be blackmail." Carol was nonplussed.

"Can you imagine my mother blackmailing her own son-in-law?"

"He was ditching her daughter."

"That was the daughter's choice."

"Maybe the mother felt vengeful and he was buying her silence."

"That's my mother you're smearing."

"Everybody's human." I reached across the table but Carol drew her hand back. This hit me the wrong way. "Quit feeling sorry for yourself. You're not the only one getting pushed around."

"What does that mean?"

"Last night someone carved up my front door with a pistol."

"For real? Why didn't you tell me?"

I bent my forefinger into a little hole and squinted through it: "I'll be curious to see if the cops think the slug's from the pistol that killed your mother."

"Can they tell that?"

"Depends on how badly the lead deforms on impact."

"Duncan, be sensible. Drop this whole stupid business. It's not worth it. You don't see the cops getting themselves shot at."

"It's true. I worry about Rachel."

"You two could stay here a few days. We could work something out."

"That's a thought. But my partner wants me back in New York."

"Maybe you should go. Let's not tempt fate." She must have read something in my face that made her add, "I love weekends in Manhattan. Or maybe you'll take me flying."

"I suppose you're right."

"You know how long it's been since I've been out in the country on a picnic for two?"

"But first I want to talk real estate with Jerry. Maybe he'll give me a crucial tip."

"You're changing your mind," she grumbled screwing the lid back on the monastic jam.

"Just till I see what's around one last corner."

▽

Chapter Twenty-Three

By overnight mail Vera sent a bundle of paperwork that kept me off the street corner till Saturday, when I packed Rachel and the pulp into the Volvo and kicked and shoved my way into Manhattan with everybody else.

After Rachel hopped out at the Museum of Natural History I doubled back uptown to Vera's. She'd taken her Ninety-sixth Street apartment as partial payment of a client's bill. We needed to refresh our parched souls at the spring of tenderness before the oasis got too crowded.

"Look at you," Vera gasped. "You've got sunlight all over your clothes. That means dangerous ultraviolet rays. Quick, peel them off. Underpants too. I'll turn the covers down."

This show of appreciation touched me—I knew perfectly well I wasn't the only prince on her parapet.

Her bedroom has a skylight. The spring sunshine celebrated her sparking curls and detected a darker brunette at the root of it. "Look at us," Vera said tossing my pants at her wicker rocking chair, "we're pale as a couple of scones. You should be ashamed, letting your health go to rot like that."

I looked at her: a solid, cocky creature shorter and

smarter than I was. But she wasn't looking at all. She was wrestling with me on the bed, going after ecstasy with the urgent cunning of a raccoon prizing open a savory trash can. She had a habit of finishing off a sentence with a quick grin for emphasis. It was no more than a tic in a way, yet I'd find myself compulsively grinning back, wrapping her in my arms.

Such is the kingdom of heaven.

Rachel came in from the museum full of new curiosity about New York. Since I'd conquered a parking space uptown, we took the subway down to Bleecker Street, where my friend Phil did specialty wind-instrument repairs in a loft big enough to house the ultralight aircraft I'd been building in two years of spare time.

It was dusky in the loft. In the shadows, with the last daylight sifting down through the skylight, the plane spread its wings from wall to wall. On Phil's workbench gleamed brass and silver tubing for trumpets and saxophones, a lathe, and metal-working tools.

Without its nylon covering the plane's lightweight tubular frame looked transparent, no more substantial than a drawing on the wall. Or as Rachel, fresh from the Museum of Natural History put it, the skeleton of a pterodactyl. Only when the lights went on did you see the pipe fitter's vise and welding equipment that made the contraption seem halfway believable. Its power plant would do just fine mowing your grass. When Rachel lighted in the canvas seat and gave the joystick a workout, the beast wagged its wings and twitched its tail. My imagination taxied across the floor and out the grimy window toward Brooklyn.

"Now if you can just perfect the rooftop takeoff," Vera said, "we can fly right over rush hour."

"Only seats one," I reminded her.
"No problem, love. I'm dieting."
"Well I'm not," Rachel countered. "Let's eat."
Which we did in an Indian restaurant on East Sixth Street, where the lamb vindaloo melts in your mouth like a Ukrainian power plant.
"Feels good to be swallowed up in the city crowds," I said. "For days I've been seeing snipers on rooftops."
"That's what his girlfriend says," Rachel chimed in. Vera seemed absorbed in the menu:
"Girlfriend?"
"Rachel means the murdered woman's daughter, Dr. Schell."
"Girlfriend?" Vera repeated.
"She's joking." I made a mental note to drop Rachel into the East River in a bag with six cats.
"If you need a murderer," Vera suggested, "your Dr. Schell sounds promising."
"If his mother-in-law threatened a scandal over his sex life, he might have a motive. But that seems pretty thin. In a state with an openly gay congressman or two, a gay lawyer can't be much of a bogeyman."
"Could the guy be chasing a buck for himself?"
"Such as?"
"Say, discounting property, then using his mother-in-law as a straw to buy it for himself."
"That would be naughty."
"Perhaps they had a spat over divvying up the profits."
"The bank estimates the property could bring five times what Dorothy O'Hare was going to pay for it. That's over a hundred thousand in profit. Would a Back Bay lawyer fight to the death over such niggling sums?"
"White-collar crime, love. You can bet he knows first-hand how hard it is to nab crooks who wear neckties."

She had a point. It takes many moons for a regulatory body to discover a dead cockroach in its coffee. And even then, it's not like a liquor-store stickup where you get prime time from the cops. Rachel turned to me.

"You already know Jerry Schell reads *The Wall Street Journal*. Maybe he's this super sleazy type."

"I'll have to ask."

Rachel tore off a spot of nan bread and began chewing: "That why you applied for that Massachusetts gun permit?"

Vera suddenly had a mouthful of porcupine quills, but she picked them out one by one without a single scream.

Chapter Twenty-Four

JERRY SCHELL SWALLOWED the whole porcupine. Tuesday noon I staked out the hall outside his office for the pleasure of his company. He was wearing his pinstriped blue lawyer uniform and toting one of those men's handbags you see in Europe. His face advertised a tanning studio, the picture of health. Until I called his name, that is. Then he swallowed the porcupine.

"I don't believe this." His face gave an ugly twist. "For the last time, I don't want to talk to you."

"I'm relieved to see you, Jerry. Your secretary told me Martians had locked you in the washroom."

"I can't take this. You and that state cop. You're hounding me, for nothing."

"Communicate with me, Jerry. How did your late mother-in-law happen to make an offer on property from an estate you happen to be liquidating?"

"I'll sue you for harassment. For defamation. Your ass will be so hung up in legal costs you won't know which end is up."

He turned sharply, trying to bulldoze me away from the open elevator door. All this childish maneuver got him was scuff marks on his pointy Italian shoes when I crammed into the elevator on his heels. We fell three floors in angry silence.

In the lobby he announced primly: "I have a lunch date."

"Look, you think I like this any more than you do?"

"I have to see this woman, a client. It's very critical."

He pushed out the revolving door looking left and right for the pumpkin coach to save him. Lunch hour scrimmaged in Marlboro Street. I said, "Level with me. Maybe I can get the troopers off your back." He hesitated long enough for me to ask, "How did Dorothy O'Hare find out about this bargain property in Dedham?"

He set out down Marlboro Street. Secretaries and classy shoppers bobbed past us on the sidewalk. In the gutter the odd pigeon bobbed for crumbs. "You've talked to Carol," he said. "You know how the old lady butted in. Push, push, push. Not just are you trying to have kids and why not, but all of it. How much did you spend on those wing-tip shoes? The works."

"It was an accident Dorothy got the house in Dedham?"

"She heard me talking about it. She made an offer. The heirs accepted it."

"Without the property ever going on the market."

"That saves a realtor's commission."

"Whose estate?"

"Olive Whitehead Carter."

"Who's that?"

"An old lady from Dover. Her father invented the automatic transmission. Or the synchronous transmission. Some mechanical thing or other."

"Rich."

"Not broke."

"Investigation will show you haven't invested a cent in the property of aforesaid rich lady?"

"That's right."
"Dorothy wasn't buying the place on your behalf."
"Of course not."
"And you never argued with her."
"No."
"Or spoiled her supper."
"Spoi—?"
"Blew her brains out."
"Ridiculous."
"I can tell the cops that."
His voice softened: "If you have to."
"They may not take my word for it."
"That's their problem," he snapped. "The sale never went through. And I never stood to profit from it anyway."

A huge moving van was backed across the sidewalk under a fancy bay window, unloading. We stepped around it into the street. Jerry Schell tried flagging a cab and looking me in the eye at the same time. "Look. I don't need this hassle." It was half plea, half rebuke, with deeper feelings waiting in the wings. "You don't understand. I let my wife go so I can be honest, quit living in lies and evasions. I do my mother-in-law a perfectly legal favor because I figure, what the hell, I've let her down. And what does it get me? More suspicions. More blame. I stand to lose so much."

He gazed up Marlboro Street as if he feared that the storefronts and the scurrying shoppers—the whole upscale kingdom—might be stage props that the movers would load into their van, piece by piece, rolling up the pavement too, until nothing remained but the sort of gorgeous, meaningless scrubland the Indians knew.

Chapter Twenty-Five

Tuesday at noon, on the nose, Phil Auburn met me at the Friendly's in Chestnut Hill. He gave me a solemn nod but no handshake, making it clear that he was there to squeeze me for information. He sat opposite me in the booth, rigid as the plastic driver of a toy car, and ordered a fishamajig sandwich on toasted white bread, skip the tartar sauce. No ketchup or salt either—bad for his high blood pressure. Since ice gave him hiccups he drank his cola straight.

"So," he said genially, "what have you got for me?"

When I told him about Dorothy O'Hare's fling in the real-estate market, he gave a little snort of satisfaction.

"Jerry Schell," I cautioned, "swears his mother-in-law found out about the Dedham property by accident."

"What do you think?"

"Do you believe in leprechauns?"

He grunted in agreement.

"In itself," I added, "it's minor-league crime."

"But not if it's a factor in a homicide. And if Schell's used inside dope to acquire some of this estate for himself, then we're talking real motives."

"He denies that."

"I'll check it out."

"I told him you would."

"Don't alarm the guy, Ames."

"He's afraid you want to nail him because he's gay."

"Uh-uh. I want to nail him because he killed his mother-in-law like you'd shoot a dog. This guy's a manipulator. A poor boy from Medford making a fast buck helping rich people inherit money they haven't earned." He frowned so that his cottony eyebrows stitched together. "That's the kind of world coming down the pike. A few slick paper pushers making millions and half the rest scrounging for handouts. No wonder kids grow up warped and lazy."

"You have kids?"

He ignored the opening. Divorced, I thought. Married to his heroic calling. From an amber prescription bottle he tapped out a Tagamet. He washed down the pill with cola, then: "We've made good progress today."

"We have?"

He slipped out his pocket notebook, keeping it close to his chest. "I talked to the victim's sister, a Mrs. Gladys Clancy from Hyde Park. On the day of the murder, she drove the victim to a Mercedes dealership on Commonwealth Ave., then to Brigham and Women's Hospital."

"Which is where I met Dorothy."

"All afternoon—got this?—Mrs. O'Hare was urging her sister to put her savings into real estate. Tremendous profits. Then they drove to the underground garage, where Mrs. O'Hare met her son-in-law for the ride home. As Mrs. Clancy left, the other two were arguing. About real estate. Schell was chewing out Mrs. O'Hare for being greedy. Mrs. Clancy heard him say, 'Pigs don't live forever.' That's a quote."

"Meaning?"

"A threat, what else? Schell drives the woman home. Half an hour later she's dead of a head wound."

"Is the American Satan a lawyer named Jerry Schell?"

"It's plausible. Would Schell fire a pistol at your front door to scare you off his tracks? I'd believe it." He slipped his notebook back into the shirt pocket of his uniform. "By the way, my ballistics people tell me the slug in your door is a twenty-two, same as the murder weapon. But it was too deformed for them to attribute it to a particular weapon."

"But why would Schell threaten Mehdi Farhat and others?"

"Maybe the Satan thing was a calculated distraction."

"That's a lot of premeditation."

"The guy's a lawyer."

"Still, that's a lot of hate."

"I've been in this business a long time."

"Where do you suppose that pistol is now?"

"If I knew, this guy would be in Walpole with a stick up his ass right this minute."

After lunch I drove over to the courthouse in Dedham to look at Olive Whitehead Carter's will. The heirs turned out to be a sister in a Lutheran nursing home in Minnesota, a handful of cousins, and several church and medical organizations. As it turned out, Olive had been sitting on parcels of land scattered all over eastern Massachusetts, from Dedham as far west as Whitinsville. Choice suburban acreage these days: a speculator's wildest dream.

Maybe it wasn't just leprechaun gold Dorothy O'Hare had promised me that afternoon in the hospital waiting room.

But time was running out for me in Boston. TV detectives never have to worry about the rent. I felt pressed to rush things, and that evening when I took Rachel in to see her mother, the pressure intensified.

"My two weeks' sick pay is up," Meg announced coolly. With help she could sit up for a few minutes at a time now. "I'll have to borrow from you to pay the bills till summer."

Not "Can you help?" but "I'll have to borrow": she was still too insecure, too proud, to show any hint of weakness. For a moment, I felt affection and anger thick as mud in my heart, and I hated the divorce that had straightened out our lives.

"A loan," I said, "is a bit ticklish. I haven't seen much income in the past few weeks."

"What about this case you're doing?"

"Limited financial rewards."

"Ah." It was a criticism. "Well, I don't have any business imposing on you anyway."

"That's true."

"You don't have to rub my face in it."

"How about asking Leon for help?"

"Waste of breath." Two months into our divorce Meg had married my former boss, only to be evicted from that bower of bliss six months later when Leon proved to have the soul of a crowbar and a lawyer to match. But that's another story. Since then she'd been selling real estate, making up slow spells by clerking in her boss's insurance agency. I bucked her up:

"You can sue the priest who whacked you."

"How do I pay the electricity in the meantime?"

"Don't worry, kid. We'll work something out."

"Then you'll help." Her hand slipped over to give mine a grateful tug.

"You don't seriously think I'd let you down, do you?"
Dearly beloved.
Lender of last resort.

At ten o'clock that night, someone fired a bullet into Mehdi Farhat's kitchen window. His housekeeper had long since left, the kids were asleep, and his security man was in bed with flu. Mehdi himself was at the kitchen table writing a letter to his brother Ari in West Germany. The bullet webbed the window glass and punctured a water pipe in the wall behind the stove. While Mehdi waited for the cops and then searched for the main water valve in the cellar, rice paddies formed on the first floor. Apparently, he was afraid to open the back door to let the flood out.

By the time I got there, after eleven, Mehdi had recovered enough to offer me a brandy while supervising the cleanup. "I was writing to my older brother—Ari is the foremost specialist of antique Oriental rugs in Freiburg, in the Black Forest. Have you ever been there? I write with a pen to show the personal respect of the old days, you understand? And I was sitting here in this chair, like this, and—!"

His larynx produced a fierce gurgle meant to signify shattering glass. His daughter Sari wandered into the room in her Care Bears nightgown, sleepy-eyed and irritable. "Is this another party? I can't sleep."

"Go put your head down," her father coaxed. "This is just an accident. This is nothing."

Chapter Twenty-Six

Sometimes a chisel will break cast iron in one blow where a hacksaw would take forever. On Thursday I decided to take mallet and chisel to Jerry Schell to see if his secrecy might crack.

On my way I picked up a telephone in a drugstore. It was a ten-dollar Singapore Special like the one upstairs at Meg's which chirped softly whenever someone dialed out on the main phone down in the kitchen. In my jacket pocket it wasn't bigger than a wallet. My battery tape recorder fit in my other pocket. I told Rachel I'd be late.

On Melrose Street at suppertime I buzzed Jerry Schell's neighbors, the amiable Beatons. We chitted and chatted, and on my way out I left a little wad of weatherstripping putty in the striker plate of the outside door.

Two minutes later I was back inside, in the cellar, where spiders had been slinging nets and mice dropping turds since Paul Revere rode by. It was restful down there. No washing machine, no workshop: nothing to bring an interruption from upstairs. The place was a dusty tomb with decrepit chairs, a birdbath, a pile of pipes and nail-studded lumber, boxes of dishes and mason jars, and a stack of old 78s.

I found the phone service lines in what had once been the coal bin. There were three old-fashioned terminals, one per apartment. With my pliers I loosened the first of them and attached my Singapore Special. Dial tone. To see if I had the right apartment I dialed Jerry Schell's number. It rang so I hung up and shifted my phone leads. This time dialing produced a busy signal: I was plugged into his line. I hung up and went upstairs to his door and knocked.

Attorney Schell was alone in the apartment. In a manner of speaking. Out of waist-high loudspeakers a plummy tenor was singing "Raindrops keep falling on my head" in stereo. A car chase was careening across the silent television screen. On the clock radio in the kitchenette a talk-show host was helping a caller see that the state's new seatbelt law was Big Government wiping out personal liberties. Papers and clothes and miscellaneous junk lay scattered about. Supper dishes stuck out of the dishwater in the kitchen sink.

My host didn't fall on me with a bear hug, but he didn't curse me either. I said, "I won't stay long." Jerry stabbed at the TV push buttons. "You leveled with me the other day," I lied, "so I feel I owe you a favor."

"Every time I see you it wrecks my day."

"And I'm sure Carol would want me to tell you."

"Tell me what?"

"I had lunch with Phil Auburn."

"The state cop."

"The same."

Jerry grimaced. No doubt he pictured me and the uniformed trooper sipping martinis in some velvet-wallpapered executive steak house. Jerry was wearing crisp new jeans and a "Purple Rain" T-shirt of the appropriate color. He said, "You tell him it was an accident, my mother-in-law buying that property?"

"Of course."

Jerry stabbed at the TV buttons. Images scrambled past. He settled for the car chase again, letting himself fall back into the sofa. "But I suppose the guy plans to have me investigated anyway."

"Uh-huh. I thought you'd want to know. He has some new evidence. There's a chance he'll book you for murder before the week is out."

On-screen a car had crashed. Jerry concentrated on the mayhem as if he hadn't heard me. But as I was about to repeat my lines he asked, "What evidence?"

"He's found a witness who heard you threaten Dorothy O'Hare the afternoon she died. I think he has sworn statements."

"That's impossible. All I ever said to her, ever, was that she was being greedy." His voice had shrunk to a tinny taped message.

"That's why I'm here. If this is a misunderstanding, you need a head start straightening it out."

"Carol send you here to warn me?"

"She thinks you're innocent."

"Of course I am. It's perfectly obvious to anybody but that cop. That fucking bigot. He'll be sorry; he'll look like such an asshole."

"You don't have access to any weapons he could connect with the murder?"

"Do I look like a gun collector?" He stared straight ahead with a sort of robotic rigidity. "What does Carol think I should do?"

"Let me put it this way. If you have something to worry about, you might try bargaining. At this stage Phil Auburn could get you a break. You want me to soften him up for you?"

"But I didn't kill the old lady," Jerry sputtered.

I shrugged: "Let me offer just one word of advice."

He glared at me. His fear glared at me. I said, "Don't get dragged off to Walpole with your heels dug in."

After a few more of these pleasantries I wrote out my phone number for him, said goodnight, and rumbled down the stairs. At the bottom I slammed the outside door and then tiptoed to the cellar door at the back of the hall.

As I was dusting a ripped kitchen chair from the junkpile, my phone began to do its cricket chirp. I picked it up, started the tape recorder, and pressed the contact mike against the earpiece. The phone rang on and on to no end. We hung up. The minute I sat down in the chair the cricket chirped again.

This time Brigham and Women's answered, and Jerry Schell pressured a succession of female voices to call Dr. Schell to the phone.

Dr. Schell was not elated. "Jerry? What are you bugging me here for? I told you, no phone calls at the hos—"

"Your friend Ames was just here warning me."

"So?"

"Okay, okay. I'm glad you sent him."

"Sent him? Listen, I can't talk now—"

"He said you'd want me to know. So I could defend myself."

She lowered her voice: "Are you stoned?"

"That state cop is trying to grab me for Dorothy's death. Ames pried it out of him today."

"Arrest you? On what evidence?"

"The afternoon Dorothy died, somebody claims they heard me threaten her. All I can think of, it must be your dippy aunt heard us and twisted my words around. She must have it in for me. Does she blame me for what happened to Dorothy?"

"Gladys is a marshmallow."

"What the hell does that mean." A demand not a question.

"Well, it's possible Gladys babbled something that's been taken the wrong way. Why should she dislike you?"

"Because she's a Boston bigot like your mother." Tension crackled on the line. Carol pushed ahead.

"If anything, Gladys would've jabbed at my mother. You know how sisters are."

"Call her up for me, will you? Find out what she said."

"Do you realize what time it is?"

"Help me, Carol. This is supposed to be an amicable divorce. We're old friends. Old partners. If it hurts me it hurts you. Right?"

"Jerry, we've been through all this. We're being better to each other now than we ever were being married."

He sighed: "Yeah yeah yeah."

"Well?" she bristled. "Am I wrong?"

"No. But this is scary. It's like she's working her hate on me from the grave."

"Take it easy."

"I know what I'm talking about. They don't even have to convict you. You can be totally innocent and they can make it impossible for the people that count even to nod to you on the street. And all the time the real—"

"Breathe slow and steady."

"Breathe, nothing. I'm not going to be everybody's scapegoat queer. No more feeling guilty and licking shit and—"

"Don't be so filthy-minded."

"Listen to you. You've shoved my face in it often enough. I gave you everything rather than—"

"Don't be so dramatic."

"I'm scared. This could be the end."

"Breathe into a paper bag so you don't hyperventilate."

"Never mind the medical rap," Jerry squawked. "I'm in real trouble, and all because—"

"Slow down, slow down. You're talking yourself into one of your panic attacks."

"If this stuff comes out, I'm finished."

"Take a couple Valiums—what've you got in the house?"

"If they try to put me in prison with a bunch of animals, I won't—"

"Stop scaring yourself silly. Every time you get into a panic spell you do something to hurt yourself."

"You tell Gladys, if I fall apart, everybody watch out." His voice was full of panicky snags, on the edge of tears.

Dr. C was firm. "Nothing's going to happen, Jerry. Unless you've done a lot worse things than I know of. Get hold of yourself."

She sounded cheerfully exasperated. Jerry kept agonizing: "If it wasn't for frigging Dorothy. If she hadn't, I mean let's face it, seeing her own death coming turned her into a frigging monster. That's what did it." His anxiety was turning into anger. "She saw her own death, and it affected her mind. And there was no reason—"

"Look, now you're blaming my mother. Leave the poor woman alone. Make sense. Go try the medicine cabinet. Or go get Larry Lollipop."

"Don't call him that. And anyway, I hardly see him anymore."

"Well, go to a movie. Get your mind off the police."

"I could use a snort."

"Be careful who you buy from," Carol said grimly, "Don't get poisoned."

"Larry's growing grass in his apartment, in a closet. He's got lights, fertilizer, the works. Maybe he'll sell me—"

"Just don't go pouring your heart out to everybody you meet. You've got enough trouble."

"After this you owe me one."

"Oh no you don't. We have a settlement and we're sticking to it." She let this sink in, then: "You'll feel better when it's all over. You'll look back and be glad we hung in there."

"It's killing me," he demanded.

"Call me at home, Jerry. Not here. Please?"

"I only—"

"It can wait. I've got a patient who—"

Anger surged in his throat: "Wait, my ass. Don't you be such a—"

He was still snapping obscenitites at her when she hung up.

I hung up. Minutes passed. More minutes passed, so I rewound the tape and sampled its mysteries. "... *Working her hate on me from the grave... seeing her own death coming turned her into a frigging monster... She saw her own death, and it affected her mind.*" Brooding over the tape in the dark I almost missed our next call.

This time soft music came on the line and a voice to match: "Hello, this is Dr. Mehdi Farhat. Unfortunately I am unable to come to the phone at this moment. However, if you will leave your name and message at the tone, I will contact you at the first moment."

At the beep Jerry Schell blurted: "It's me. Jerry Schell. I really have to see you." He was so flustered he hung up without leaving his phone number.

At a quarter to eleven he dialed another number and

asked for Morris. Whoever he was, Morris was overwhelmed to hear from "Cherry" Schell. Couldn't complain about business. Was indignant to hear about the police harassment Cherry was putting up with.

"What a farce!" Jerry exploded. "This cop with his head up his ass, having so much power. Looking for a scapegoat. And I have to defend myself."

"Of course you do," Morris agreed. "There ought to be a public fund for businesses to defend themselves from malicious allegations. You have to hit them right back. Threaten to sue. Look at me and that Teawater Woods Development."

"At least the DEQE's in place."

"Nothing to worry about there, Cherry. Take my word."

"I never expected. You worry and worry, and in the end they hang you for something you never did."

"Nah, it's not the end. You take it too much to heart. You got to be more philosophical."

They discussed philosophy.

After we hung up I sat in the dark for twenty minutes. Water rushed in the pipes as people got ready for bed. Then my phone chirped again. This time we tapped an elderly female voice: a sleepy, alarmed hello.

"Gladys, it's me. Jerry Schell."

"Who?"

"Carol's husband."

Gladys died.

"I'm calling . . . I wanted to ask you, remember the afternoon I gave Dorothy a lift home?"

Gladys went silently to heaven.

"I hope I didn't wake you. It's just that I, this state trooper, a guy named Auburn, he's telling people that you heard me threaten Dorothy the day she died. Is that true?"

"Well, I— What time is it?"

"He claims you overheard me threaten Dorothy's life."

"Oh dear, no. I mean, I did mention how you two were disagreeing about something. That's all. And of course you called Dorothy a pig."

"Exactly. 'Don't be a pig,' I told her. See, she made a bid on part of an estate I was handling. I talked the heirs into giving her a good deal to save them time and expenses. But see, it could be made to look like I was defrauding the estate. I had to be careful. And she was getting greedy, she was pressuring me to let her buy mo—"

A new voice crashed the party, an irate male voice raised half a waspy octave by old age: "Jesus S. Christ, it's the middle of the night."

"Oh, it's you, Mr. Clancy. Sorry. It's just me, Carol's husband."

"That's ancient history."

"I was trying with your wife to clear up—"

"Do you know what time it is?"

"I'm sorry, but this isn't a triv—"

"Gladys just got over the shingles. We have a bad enough time getting our sleep without you upsetting her."

Jerry dug in: "She's the source of a dangerous misunderstanding, and I'm—"

"Shingles leaves pain in your fingers and toes. You understand me?"

"She's—"

"So you're causing her pain, you hear me?"

Jerry fought back: "Gladys is accusing me . . . I'm sure it's all a misunderstanding, but it's very serious—"

"You people are pushy as hell, is what you are."

"Put Gladys back on the phone for two minutes."

"Don't push me around," he barked.
"Please just put her—"
"Do I have to call the goddamn police?"
We all hung up more or less at once.

Five minutes later footsteps clattered in the hallway overhead. The Purple Rain T-shirt went by the cellar window. I wasn't prepared for excursions.

No time to disconnect the phone. In fact in my shortcut to the stairs I kicked an empty olive-oil tin that marched across the floor like a drum and bugle corps. On my way out I had to chance packing the door latch with weatherstripping putty again.

Captain Nemo's was twenty thousand leagues under the sea: a basement bar flooded by blue light. Inside the lava lamps on each table, immiscible blobs did an imitation of rippling red tongues or the tube worms that shimmy in the volcanic canyons at the bottom of the sea. The crowd was a mix of old friends and lonesome Petes, and a few predictable freaks, including a pair of James Dean blonds joined at the earlobes by lengths of gold chain tied together like a fancy curtain tassel.

Jerry Schell cruised the patrons trying to score some coke or dope. Larry was there. Jerry hugged him, nesting his chin on Larry's shoulder; then he moved on to the pay phone. After the call he knocked off a double scotch at the bar and shot back up to the street. As far as I could tell no pharmaceuticals had changed hands.

We walked. We cruised the combat zone, ducking into a club where the stripper had a droopy belly and skin the color of chicken fat. Out on Tremont Street we passed college kids and bored cops. He cruised Boston Common looking for Cupid in the vicinity of men's rooms and benches, or maybe just afraid to go back home alone.

Once he stopped to flop in the black grass under the random stars. I watched him across the lawn. No one mugged him. No one arrested him. No one asked what miracle he was hoping for.

We took the long way back, across Stuart Street, past the old Statler Hotel, where Legal Seafood is now. No one had sold Jerry any bliss.

In the dusty cellar on Melrose Street I put three chairs side by side and stretched out. To keep awake I replayed the taped phone calls. In the darkness the voices buzzed in the earphone, distinct and meaningless as the noises you'd hear beyond you all night in Vietnam: bats and rats and a million insects. *Turned her into a frigging monster. She saw her own death, and it affected her mind.* Dorothy O'Hare with fangs and blood-red runny eyes. Dorothy O'Hare with horns.

Then I was cutting through an alley behind a trolley barn—you could see the orange streetcars lined up inside—and the brick wall began to lean into me. It was falling, pushing me off balance, cracking up. I shoved against the bricks with all my might, inching forward, hoping I could hold the wall up long enough to get out from under. It was crushing the left side of my body when I woke up aching on the three chairs in the cellar on Melrose Street. Dawn was leaking into the cellar windows. A toilet flushed above me.

People went off to work. No sign of Jerry Schell. I began to think I'd missed him: that the early bird was out getting a head start on his legal worm. After a while I rang his doorbell—to no avail. A garbage truck grunted along the narrow street outside. I found myself wondering if Jerry Schell's personal finances had left a paper trail in his rooms upstairs.

By unlocking the window in the upstairs hall, a visitor could step out onto the fire escape and then into the kitchen window next door. Overnight the dishwater had drained out of the sink leaving yesterday's dishes marked by rings of grease. On a peg hung an apron with a cartoon bull saying, "Now you're cookin'. " The lights were on upstairs. I went up the steep staircase. A Purple Rain T-shirt, jeans, and striped boxer shorts lay rumpled in a corner of the bedroom. The bathroom occupied an odd-shaped nook with a roof window and a water-splashed tile floor. Behind the door was a bathtub full of chilly water and dead lawyer.

Jerry Schell was lying on his side in the tub, right arm up and dangling over the rim, as if demonstrating the Australian crawl. His skin had a bluish pallor. The fluorescent light picked out a bald spot at his crown. At his feet the chrome spout dripped. The water was cold. You could have assumed he was stoned if his nose and one half-open eye had not slipped below the waterline.

He'd been dead several hours, I guessed. Coronary trouble perhaps. No pill bottles, no indications of violence. As I was pondering the problem the doorbell rang.

How could I explain my presence here? I shot down the banister to the living room and looked out. In the street sat a patrol car, its red bubble silently spinning.

Time to call the police.

No sooner had I snatched up the phone and dialed 911 than a voice from the kitchen invited me to freeze. I obliged. Without turning around—few things on this earth are more dangerous than a frightened male with a service revolver—I said, "I'm just phoning for an ambulance. Mr. Schell's apparently had a heart attack."

"Who are you? A neighbor?"

We faced each other. Bepimpled lad in a crisp new uniform. He held the revolver so rigid he might have been in a window at Filene's. The other cop banged on the hall door and yelled. I stepped over to let him in. He had wide black shoes and extra chins and worried eyes. The pimpled lad said, "We got a call about a prowler out on the fire escape."

"That was me," I offered. "I had an appointment with Mr. Schell this morning, and when he didn't answer the door I got worried. Look."

The three of us trooped upstairs to inspect the swimmer. The older of the two cops felt for a pulse, then shook his head. "No hurry on the wagon."

The younger one drew back: "Awful young for a heart attack. Probably never exercised."

I suggested nobody touch the body until we could get Phil Auburn here. This bit of advice called for introductions and explanations. I handed out my business card. "Mr. Schell's been under investigation. His mother-in-law was murdered out in Newton a couple weeks ago."

My helpfulness backfired, since now the two of them took steps to secure the apartment. This kept me from ducking out to ditch telephone and tape recorder in the Volvo. Wiretapping is a federal no-no, with strong negative incentives. To play it safe I pocketed the cassette, then wiped the recorder on my pantleg and let it drop behind the couch cushions, where it became part of Jerry Schell's estate. Ditto the phone.

Phil Auburn opened with his usual line: "So what have you got for me, Ames?"

"You sound like a collection agent."

He was offended: "Well, what the hell are you doing here?"

"When I talked to Jerry Schell last night, he seemed spaced out. Then this morning I couldn't rouse him. I got concerned."

"You broke into his house."

"I try to be a good neighbor."

To the cops he said, "Keep Mr. Ames here."

Phil Auburn went upstairs to appreciate the dead man and explore. Not ten minutes later he came down delicately toting a pistol. He carried it upended by means of a toothbrush stuck up its muzzle so as not to muddle any fingerprints. It was a target pistol, a Ruger .22 modeled on the Colt .45. A taste of the frontier for city slickers. Though Phil Auburn tried to look solemn, his face gleamed with triumph.

I was relieved. Partly because the pistol released me from suspicion. Or so I thought until he asked, "Where were you last night?"

"Here on Melrose Street. Staking out Schell. Around midnight he took a stroll to Captain Nemo's down the street. Tried to corner some dope. Walked over to the Common. Came back just after one. I tailed him, then I napped in my car."

"How come you didn't get a ticket parked in tow zone?"

"Bad luck."

"Uh-uh, my friend." Lieutenant Auburn shook his head. "I spotted your car out here—it's that old Volvo, isn't it? It was tagged at two-thirty A.M. in the middle of the night, just about the time—I'll bet anything—just when Schell died. And you wouldn't have gotten the ticket if you'd been out there in it."

I shrugged: "I spent the night in the cellar. I can show you the chair I slept on."

"It makes more sense you were in this apartment."

Phil Auburn waved me into the kitchen, out of earshot: "How do I know you didn't kill Schell? I mean, who the hell are you really?"

I scanned his face for some sign that he was joking.

"How do I know you didn't feed him an overdose of something?" He rubbed the spot between his bushy brows with his fingertip, like a psychic summoning inspiration. "Suppose Schell was paying you off. Suppose he put you onto properties he couldn't buy in his own name. And suppose the mother-in-law found out. So one of you killed her. And then last night somebody panicked."

"You're giving me an idea."

"From the start you've tried to get Schell off the hook."

"It may be the truth."

"Not likely. See this? This is a pistol. I found it hidden in the back of his closet up there. I bet Dorothy O'Hare would recognize it. I bet it's the last thing she ever saw."

"Maybe it fired at my front door the other night."

The bushy brows frowned. "Maybe Schell got tired of your blackmail. For that matter, maybe you fired at your own door to put off suspicion."

"You're full of stimulating ideas."

"You better come into the office."

Chapter Twenty-Seven

The guest room in the state police barracks came with a conference table big enough for billiards, a green blackboard, and walls yellow as an old dog's molars.

We ran around in circles together, with time out for a couple phone calls to New York soliciting character references for me. After a couple hours of this we ate take-out burgers (for him, two on one bun, no ketchup). Then Phil Auburn called the police lab. He liked what he heard: "It's an old Ruger target pistol, a series from the mid-fifties. Two spent shells in the cylinder."

"One for Dorothy O'Hare and one for my front door. Or Dr. Farhat's."

"You count good."

"Where's the other one?"

"Probably the weapon's been reloaded."

"What do they say about the fingerprints?"

"They look to be Schell's. Fresh ones, very distinct. Some bluing's very sensitive to skin oils."

"Or someone put the gun in the wet hand of a dead Schell. Then hid it where even a cop could find it."

"The ex-wife tells me the guy pestered her over the

phone last night. He sounded shook up about our investigation and kept dropping hints about substance abuse."

I was tempted to play him my tape of The Lawyer's Lullaby, but his attitude put me off.

As I was being dismissed an hour later, the preliminary autopsy report came in. Coronary collapse with indications of toxic insult, source undetermined. Lab reports pending.

But where had the stuff come from? Jerry Schell's cupboard was bare. And on our Boston-by-moonlight walking tour I hadn't seen any ecstatic substances change hands. So I was missing something, but what? Phil Auburn clucked gravely:

"There's this new garbage cocaine in Boston this spring. Laced with some solvent. Methyl-something. They're dropping like flies out there. Especially the black junkies in Roxbury, they'd eat dog doo off your lawn. The stuff's everywhere, cheap as rain. How much you want to bet that's our culprit?"

I started for the door. He reminded me, "Don't make me have to go looking for you. You force me to get official with you, you won't like it. Believe me."

"It was my fault," Carol confessed. "Jerry got me on the phone last night and unloaded on me. I thought he was just being paranoid. So I brushed him off by telling him to take a Valium and cool it."

We had ducked into a staff room at the hospital. It had a green blackboard like the room in which I'd spent the morning, only here someone had chalked up a diagram of a heart that resembled an onion leaking tear-shaped drops. Carol sat across the table scratching at her clipboard and watching me eat a roast-beef grinder. She was reaching the end of a twenty-four-hour shift, and her eyes showed it. Tears hadn't helped.

"You were about to divorce the guy," I said. "Why did he keep leaning on you?"

"Who do you turn to when you're flipped out? The wife. Doctor. Mommy." She shook her head guiltily. "I should've known he'd hurt himself. I could see it coming. Sometimes I stink as a doctor. But I was annoyed with him bugging me, so I brushed him off."

Her eyes grew shiny with pain. I kept pressing: "Did Jerry have a bad back?"

"Not that I know of. Why?"

"Just curious. How close are you to his pal Larry Lollipop?"

She was faked out: "How did you know I called Larry that?"

I lied: "I heard Jerry use that name."

"His name's Larry Lillo. He's the one who tipped me off that Jerry'd had himself tested for AIDS. Larry had an emergent case of hepatitis last year. We had a sweet relationship in the hospital, Larry and me. Nothing sexy." She hesitated: "I never had a brother."

"Do you know a friend of Jerry's named Morris?"

"Just Morris Field. They were business friends. Morris does real estate."

"Morris was in trouble with the law a while back?"

"I guess so. It was something ambiguous. Different readings of a deed or a regulation or something. Anyway, they tried to prosecute him."

"Tried?"

"Well, he's not in jail, is he?"

The roast beef in the grinder could have been rawhide. I chewed faster: "So what was Jerry so uptight about?"

Carol sucked in some breath: "Superficially, business. He seemed scared they'd find out about my mother buying that two-family in Dedham."

"But why panic? If the regulatory bodies don't even yip at the millionaire looters, why worry about chicken feed? Would the heirs sue him? Or was Jerry also investing for himself on the sly?"

"I'm divorcing the man. I'm the last person he'd tell." Suddenly her eyes met mine: "He told me you'd been threatening him. Warning him that he was about to be arrested."

"I only told him what I knew."

"Oh?" She gave me a dangerous stare. "I had the impression you wanted to scare him to death. And you finally did."

The force of her anger knocked easy answers off my tongue. I said, "Let's not make a saint of him so soon."

"I had the impression you were frustrated and out for blood. This Lieutenant Auburn didn't say anything about an indictment."

"What do you expect the cops to tell you?"

"The truth. More than I get from you. Jerry told me you were trying to scare him, claiming I sent you to warn him."

I had one of those moments in which totally incompatible realities shimmer in your head. I had pushed an innocent man to suicide, and the guilt was about to suffocate me. Or he had died the victim of a drug accident or murder. I hated my reaction even as it slipped off my tongue: "You married Jerry when you were in tough shape in med school. Depressed and broke."

"So?"

"So one reason you take the divorce so calmly is that you felt guilty and phony about the marriage all along."

"That's pretty low, Duncan. Rather than face a bad mistake you blame me. I'm glad you're not a surgeon."

"The fact is, you were glad to be let out of a phony marriage. With face saved and a decent cash settlement."

Her eyes despised me and I couldn't help it. "Even if that were true," she said, "it wouldn't excuse driving someone to suicide."

"Would you call him suicidal?"

Her knuckles drummed on the tabletop: "Jerry—in my eyes anyway—Jerry never actually came out of the closet. He could never decide who he wanted to be. This grabby guy, you'd be jammed together in an elevator on a date, and he'd slide his knee between your legs and half hump you there like he owned you. Like he couldn't resist. But then once when we were yelling at each other, he picked up one of my bras like it was a spider and—"

She broke off with a little groan. I said, "But you loved him."

"Behind the scary part of him, the mask part, he was a sweet little boy. Part of him was always behind the closet door listening to the action out here, spying through the crack. I'm no psychiatrist."

"I should tell you. The cops found a pistol in the Melrose Street apartment. It may be the weapon that killed Dorothy."

Carol sank back in her chair. Out on the corridor PA system a Southie accent was paging a Dr. Mahvin. Finally Carol said, "I guess I was afraid of something like that."

"You knew he had the pistol?"

She was grimly scraping her pencil against the edge of the clipboard, back and forth. "The evidence kept closing in. It's too painful to absorb all at once."

"I know. It doesn't feel right. Jerry was sure as hell

guilty of something, maybe a lot of things. But not Dorothy's murder."

"What about the pistol?"

"It doesn't feel right."

"It doesn't feel right," she echoed. "Do you realize how feeble that sounds?"

"I realize."

"Well, I hope you're right. But a physician who said that would be laughed off the floor."

Chapter Twenty-Eight

I FOUND LARRY LILLO off Central Square in Cambridge, up the street from a forgotten-looking Greek Orthodox church. Larry's corner of the block had recently been cleared by fire to make room for a brick apartment building functional as a Soviet toolshed.

"It's unlocked!" Larry shouted. He met me with plastic-coated executive dumbbells in each hand. He was barechested, wearing sweatpants, unsoiled running shoes, and wavy blond hair. I shook hands with his dumbbell.

Instead of a coffee table, a workout bench dominated the living room. On the vinyl couch were leather straps, iron shoes, squeezy exercisers for gripping and bear hugging, a yellow tape measure, and one ten-pound barbell plate sinking into the soft seat cushion as if it would eventually fall through the floor into the cellar.

Out from behind the couch waddled a small bulldog with clipped ears, eyeteeth, and jowls that drooped like melting cheese. He stationed himself between his master's legs and offered me a burping growl. Larry growled too: "Quiet Duke."

They stood their ground, the two of them, Larry's right

hand grimly working the Vita Torsion Steel Grip Exerciser. It squeaked.

"I take it you've seen the evening news," I began.

"I never watch the news," he said somewhat sniffily. "It's bad for you to get dosed by depressive input day after day."

"Your friend Jerry Schell died last night."

"Yeah, I heard."

"Drug overdose."

"Yeah, I heard."

"Maybe you also heard that he tried to buy some happiness from you at Captain Nemo's around midnight."

"Where'd you get that input?"

"I witnessed it."

"What were you doing there?"

"Scouting for Santa. Seeing who's naughty and nice."

"Well I didn't give Jerry any substances." Larry's confidence was sinking like the barbell weight on the couch.

"Where did you go after you left Captain Nemo's?"

"Home." He hit the correction button: "After I stopped by a friend's place. I can prove that."

"You and Jerry were real close for a while."

"His wife terminated that."

"She likes you."

"She was tired of Jerry. I was a good excuse for her to write him off."

"You were all friends?"

"We played tennis together. Played a little racquetball. Jerry was never in that great a shape."

"Is that why he went to Mehdi Farhat, the chiropractor?"

"I don't have any input on that."

"Try."

"I don't like being monitored."

"Jerry do any business with Mehdi Farhat?"

"I have no data on that—and definitely not for you."

I stepped quickly into the kitchen. Larry tossed the Vita Torsion Steel Grip Exerciser onto the couch and tried to cut me off.

"What are you looking for?"

"For one thing, a glass of water." I pushed into the kitchen and let the water run in the sink. Next to the stove was a door leading perhaps to a pantry or laundry room. A nickel-plated hasp and padlock advertised its significance. A laundry room would have handy connections for lights and water.

Larry shoved a glass at me. "Drink it and get out."

"Mmm. My green thumb is beginning to throb. There must be a greenhouse nearby."

The message got through. Larry shook his head in disgusted disbelief. I said, "What could it be? Any potted petunias in the house?"

His eyes followed mine to the laundry-room door. I glanced around the kitchen to be sure there were no sharp implements handy to help him express his frustration. From the strainer basket in the sink I took a butter knife, then I strode to the door and went to work. Larry decided to butt in: "What are you doing with the knife?"

"Unscrewing his hasp. It's installed wrong. It's supposed to fold over the screws so no intruder can grab a butter knife and do what I'm doing. I'll show you."

"Leave it alone."

"And these cheap riveted padlocks are feeble anyway."

"Get away from there."

"Tut-tut. You don't want to be careless about security. You'll have strangers endangering your secrets." The first screw came out of the cheesy luan door. "Boy, is my thumb throbbing. Something's growing around here."

This commotion brought the bulldog waddling into the kitchen. I admired his tusks.

"I'm warning you." Larry grabbed my jacket's sleeve with both hands, holding rather than ripping. His new Torsion Steel grip instantly subdued the wool. The second screw pattered onto the vinyl floor, and I started on the third one. Larry weighed the urge to triumph against the certainty of pain, then released my sleeve.

"Don't step on that screw," I said. "You'll mark up your floor."

The hasp came loose. The bulldog waddled into the doorway.

"What were you saying about Jerry's connection to Mehdi Farhat?"

"What do I know?" Larry complained. "Jerry gave the guy money. Sometimes Jerry put money in my account, and I'd have to withdraw cash to give to Farhat."

"How much? Hundreds?"

"Why is this so important?" he pleaded.

"Take my word for it."

"I suppose with Jerry gone there's no reason for secrecy anymore."

"What kind of numbers are we talking about?"

"Sometimes thousands. Sometimes tens of thousands. It bugged me. The IRS had already gotten on me about some deductions I took when I first went to work at Raytheon. I don't want another audit."

"I thought you were a lab technician at the hospital."

He scoffed: "I was in the hospital with hepatitis for a few weeks last fall. Him and me, we were hanging out together at his place, and his wife comes in and stares at my yellow eyeballs and says I'm jaundiced, it's serious, you better get into the hospital fast. She scared me half to death; I thought it was something fatal."

"AIDS."

"Something fatal."

"So you warned her Jerry might have the disease."

"You heard about that." He was rattled. "Carol was one of the doctors on my case, see. And when I got better I had this fantastic reaction to her. Like she saved my life. The way you feel about the saints when you're a kid. Like, she fills you with this power. Some solar collector inside you starts charging like you're finally alive. In the hospital that last week, me and her, we were like this." His hands gripped each other tight. "Ama-a-a-zing."

"You were lovers?"

"Just about. Don't get the wrong idea. I'm not gay. I go with whatever relationship happens to be best at the time." A boyish grin flashed in and out of focus on his face. "But it wrecked everything for her and Jerry. And for me and him too."

"What do you do for Raytheon?"

"Right now, SDI contracts. I do computer simulations of extreme physical-stress situations. Like rocket lift-offs. Or explosions. In and out of terrestrial environments. It's heavy theory," he said with gentle condescension. "You wouldn't understand it."

"How'd you ever get a security clearance?"

He couldn't suppress a grin: "I got a degree in math. You wouldn't believe how straight I used to be. And this is Star Wars contracts we're talking. Big money. Billions, over years and years. They'd give Khaddafy a clearance if he had the right technical specialty. Me, I know how to sell a proposal. I do big color charts, numbers, arrows, everything. See, the idea is, you have to get the spending momentum up, then—"

"So why was Jerry laundering payments to Mehdi Farhat?"

"It was supposed to be repaying loans. Farhat paid the bills for Carol's medical school. It wasn't any of my business."

"That's because your thumb didn't throb like mine."

"Wait—"

I pulled on the door. Inside the laundry room under cheery metal halide grow lights were greenhouse pots sitting in trays of water. Out of the pots sprang Jack's beanstalks. Most of the plants reached up into the light fixtures, where timers faked the heavenly rhythms of sun and moon. Against the wall stood a torpedo-shaped CO_2 cylinder with a homemade valve to waft gas over the beanstalks. Above it on a shelf sat the ballasts for the lights. Aluminum foil papered the walls with glare, and the air smelled of sweet tropical summer. Stretch out in a hammock and shut your eyes and you could be in Tahiti.

"High-tech agriculture," I said. "It figures."

"The botany's really interesting. But the hardware's simple. You buy these hydroponic nutrient mixes from Holland and seeds from California." Larry began to expatiate on the relationship of carbon dioxide and proportional darkness to the sex life of the marijuana plant. Surveying his garden kingdom, he couldn't deny his pride in his work.

"You must be making big bucks in Star Wars," I said. "What are you doing peddling this weed?"

"I don't sell it," he protested. "Me and a friend or two, just being sociable, we can smoke this little crop. If there's a quarter-pound here, I'll be lucky."

"A victory garden."

"You have to protect yourself. What with the government spraying herbicides on the Mexican crop and all, you're just asking for cancer. You're just sucking in Agent Orange. It's Vietnam all over again."

"Were you in Vietnam?"

"I was still in high school."

"Then I wouldn't make speeches about Vietnam."

He was eager not to offend me now. "All I meant was, you have to defend yourself."

"So they tell me. If you want to stay defended, you'll find me the check registers that show the sums Jerry Schell deposited for Dr. Farhat."

"What if I scratched that old data?"

"Then the harvest may come early this year."

"I'll initiate a search."

I left him sulking in the doorway, the porky Duke between his master's legs with his pink tongue dangling. Larry stood there flexing his bare chest a bit, thumbs hooked in the waistband of his baggy sweatpants: Sinbad the Sailor in the forbidden gardens of Babylon.

Chapter Twenty-Nine

As on my last midnight visit to Mehdi Farhat's, cars jammed the driveway and the house was lit up like a cruise liner. But this time the cars were Caddies, not cop machines, and designer guests flooded the downstairs rooms.

Mehdi's security man, a bug-eyed and self-important former warehouse watchman, stopped me on the sidewalk. He called up to the house on his walkie-talkie to authorize my entry.

His Excellency, Prince Duncan of Natick.

The event was a political fund-raiser for the homeless that an hour earlier had briefly showcased a campaigning junior Kennedy. Also, I was told I'd missed a very tasteful belly dancer and her trio. Now just before midnight Mehdi was still following his handshake from room to room, praising everyone, connecting this one and that. He wore a sleeveless cashmere sweater over his Italian dress shirt to complement pin-striped trousers suitable for a treaty signing.

"I don't want to crash your party," I said.

"Come in, Duncan. People will be interested in your work. You can make some contacts."

It was a mixed crowd, peacocks and churchmice, executive privilege and just folks. Even a couple of black faces. "In America," Mehdi beamed, "people volunteer to help. Do you know how amazing that is other places in the world? This is a wonderful country."

The buffet table offered a roast beef, a pineappled ham, and a turkey. You could thrust with your own blade, or ask the bow-tied kid with the electric knife to attack in your name.

Despite the steady scrimmage at the bar the fund-raisers seemed to be a sober bunch. But there were exceptions. At one point, a couple of sports—one a gray-haired America's Cup backer—dodged through the party shooting each other with the look-alike Beretta pistols I'd seen Sari playing with. Every so often the buzzer announced a kill. They twisted and whooped through this survival course, proving that raising money for the homeless doesn't have to be dull.

"Everybody loves those guns." Mehdi shuddered.

He began introducing me around the room as a New York security consultant—faster than a speeding bullet and able to leap tall buildings.

After this advertising blitz and a couple of scotches I managed to hip-check him into the little den off the kitchen. Sari and her older brother George were watching rock videos on a mini TV. Mehdi shooed them off to bed. I broke the news:

"Dorothy O'Hare's son-in-law died last night. Apparently of a drug overdose."

He winced: "Jerry Schell was a patient of mine. Last night he left a message on my answering machine. The office girl found it this morning."

"What do you suppose he wanted?"

"He suffered from stress. Terrible stress. We were doing stress-reduction work."

"He's been making regular payments to you."

"Well, sometimes we set up a treatment program for patients who need long-term therapy."

"We're talking thousands of dollars."

"I'd have to look up the records."

"Wouldn't insurance have paid for his treatments?"

"Sometimes no. The pill pushers, the AMA, they hound the insurance companies not to pay chiropractic specialists. The government too. It hurts to think of all the poor people who suffer because welfare won't cover our services." He waved his hand indignantly. "We're health professionals, we—"

"You're going to have investigators demanding to look at those records. They may wonder if you've been buying real estate with tips from your friends."

Mehdi looked hurt and mystified. He turned off the TV video: "I paid many of the bills for Carol's medical school."

"She never told me."

"Mrs. O'Hare was a proud woman. Her daughter too. That's the Irish, as you say. And it was Jerry's personality to insist that he would pay back the money. Jerry was kind of a—what's the word—a feudal person, like in the old country. As if, if he owed you, you owed him. So he had to pay everything back. You understand?"

"I'm sure Carol's grateful to you."

"Isn't she admirable?" He accented the *mire*: ad-*mire*-able.

We both beamed. "So tell me," I asked, "why did Jerry pass the cash to you through his friend Larry?"

"I don't know any Larry."

"Lawrence T. Lillo. He claims he made cash payments to you a few months ago."

"Does he have proof?"

"Too soon to say."

He smiled: "Ah. You see?"

"Reassure me. Tell me you've never bought any part of the Olive Whitehead Carter estate."

"Duncan," he groaned. "Why would I buy part of this lady's estate?"

"Because some of the land she owned is a gold mine."

"I invest in real estate, business. I'm planning a complex in the town of Norwood. Spirit Plaza. It will have more square feet of glass than—"

"The cops are going to want to know where you were last night around three A.M."

"Me?"

"They're wondering where the fatal drug came from. And you were one of the people Jerry phoned."

"But I always discourage my patients away from chemicals." He shook his head: "The man is dead. Why do they make a big investigation?"

"For one thing, they found a pistol in his apartment."

"Not—?"

"Possibly."

Mehdi let out a mighty sigh, as you'd do if you caught a baseball bat in the midriff. He took my arm. "Your glass is empty. Even I may drink some alcohol tonight."

We headed for the bar. I said, "And by the way, where were you last night?"

"Here in my house of course."

"You can prove that? In case the cops push you?"

He thought a minute. "Sari woke up with a bad dream just after three o'clock. We looked at her clock together."

"The question is, will she be able to explain that to the police."

"Why don't you ask her?" He pointed to the staircase. "I have to say good-bye to some guests."

I paused to admire the carpet on the wall, with its splendid tree of paradise, then I went upstairs.

Sari was in bed reading with a rechargeable flashlight which she ditched under her pillow when I tapped on the half-open door. "It's me," I said. "Duncan."

"My father lets me read," she said defiantly.

"What's the book?"

She flashed a horror comic. Rotting corpses chasing dewy-eyed blondes. I said, "Looks scary."

"They're cute," she said with the same edge of defiance.

I stuck to my guns: "I'd be scared."

"Watch this." She stuck the flashlight under her chin so that its rays exaggerated the deformity of her nose and mouth. Her face seemed to be collapsing around huge, ghoulish eye sockets. Knowingly, almost daring me, she said, "Pretty horrible, huh?"

"Shall I try too?"

"Carol's going to have the doctors fix it when I'm in eighth grade." *It.* "Your bones have to be grown in."

"You miss your mother?"

She shook her head: "My mother dropped me out the window on my face. That's why she lives so far away."

"Who told you that?"

"Don't you like this guy with the hundred eyes all over his body?" She waved the comic book: "And this one has—"

"Was Dorothy O'Hare kind of your mother?"

"Ugh. Too-o-o bossy. We used to hide."

"Who's we?"

"Me and Carol. Carol brings me comics. She gave me Galgen."

Galgen was a stuffed creature something like an octopus, with hilarious goggle eyes and a nasty beaked mouth. Sari hugged it dearly. I said, "Was Carol invited tonight?"

"I asked my dad to call her. Maybe she's sleeping at the hospital. When you're a doctor you sleep there sometimes."

"You like her."

"She's my best mother. I want her to marry my dad."

"He says you woke up with a bad dream last night."

"Yeah, it was ten past three."

"You remember that?"

"He showed me on the clock." She pointed to the luminous Mickey Mouse clockface on her nightstand. "I don't remember the dream though."

"You'd better get some sleep. You're up real late."

"I'm staying up till midnight."

"It's already past midnight."

"No it isn't."

I showed her my watch. That was when I noticed her clock was an hour slow. "Have you changed the time setting?"

"Uh-uh. My dad will buy a new one."

"Nobody's touched it as far as you know?"

"Would you tell my father I want a drink of water?"

"Let me ask you a question first."

But at that point George rumbled into the hall: "Hey come *on*, you guys. How's anyone supposed to sleep around here with you two yapping all the time."

And an instant later Mehdi was on the stairs. "So. Did you find out what you wanted?"

Sari scuttled out of bed and piled into her father: "My clock's a whole hour wrong."

Mehdi pushed past her. "Aha," he cried, poking fun.

"In that case we need to throw it out and buy a new one." He pulled the plug out of the wall and held up the clockface dangling by the cord like a headhunter displaying an enemy: "Into the trash barrel with you."

"But wait—" Sara objected.

"Oh no no," he insisted. "Let's get this junk out of the house."

Downstairs guests were still assaulting the turkey cadaver. The crystal chandelier spattered everybody with sequins of light. I took a final suck of scotch, then I pulled my rip cord.

Stars mobbed the spring sky. The air smelled of worm-turned loam and cut grass. Mehdi's security man was slouched in his Pontiac busting a six-pack as I went by.

It bothered me that Sari's clock told the wrong time. Suppose a conscientious health professional had paid a house call in the middle of the night, bringing his patient lasting relief. Suppose he woke Sari afterward, told her she'd been dreaming, and showed her the clock. Under these circumstances he might never get credit for relieving Jerry Schell's suffering.

I strolled over to the office building, admiring the alarm system I'd helped him choose, wondering if Mehdi kept records that would repay some personal research.

Behind the offices the moonlight burned blue on the roof of the barn housing the ancient fire engines. As I rounded the corner a ghost floated across the moonlit lawn from the street.

"Carol."

She pulled up short: "Duncan, is that you?"

"Come to see your favorite fire engine?"

"There's a party. I'm late, I just got off duty."

"I didn't realize Mehdi'd invited you."

She gave a shy shrug: "My mother used to say Mehdi was a little sweet on me. Are you here to party too?"

"I dropped by to dance and eat turkey and mention that Jerry was dead. The next thing I knew, Mehdi was telling me he covered some of your tuition at Tufts, and Jerry was paying off the loan. And I wondered, how come Carol hasn't brought up this stuff."

"I thought we repaid Mehdi ages ago."

"How much money are we talking about?"

"I'm not sure exactly."

"And why was Jerry making the payments?"

"I was just starting my residency at the hospital then. I was swamped. The debt was just a nuisance."

"Look. Your mother was using your husband's inside data to rack up a fat real-estate deal. She was working for Dr. Farhat. Now I hear that Jerry passed funds to Dr. F on the sly. It makes you wonder."

"I don't care."

"I bet I know some prosecutors who might."

"They can't do anything to Jerry now."

"Jerry's dead. Your mother's dead."

"You shit." She burst into angry tears. "I was trying to be honest with you. I said I don't care. And not because I'm insensitive. What do I care about my mother's money schemes? God, I never even balance my checkbook."

"Not so loud," I tried to slip my arm around her. "Mehdi's watchman is out front in his car."

"You bully me. You bully me about not having feelings while you go around trying to bash things open. That's funny. That's hilarious."

"Take it easy."

"I will not take it easy." She stormed off. I caught her by the shoulders and pulled her to me. Her fist thumped my breastbone. It sounded like someone punching a phone book. We both froze. After a while, she pressed her nose against my hard collarbone. On my skin I could feel tears, the genuine wet article.

We moved under the shed roof, where the old horse-drawn pumper stood. Its brass fittings gleamed in the blackness. With my arms full I leaned back against a huge wooden wheel. Iron springs creaked in the dark. "Mehdi's been so good to me," Carol said. "If he's involved in this mess, I'll die."

"I have to check out every tunnel."

"Please don't let Larry trick you. Ever since Jerry dropped him, he's been bitchy. That's the only trouble with strange relationships like that. They get so vindictive."

"Sari says you're at her house all the time. Her second mother."

"Sari and I were together a lot when my mother was working here. The kid's been so isolated. And terrified of the plastic surgery she needs. So much depends on it. I took her into Children's Hospital for the surgical evaluation."

"What happened to her? She blames her mother."

"It's a birth injury. Nobody's fault. But her mother ran out just after Sari was born. She runs a string of hair salons in Los Angeles. Sari's never forgiven her. Except when she's mad at her father. Then her mother's the saint."

"Sari expects you to marry her father."

Carol gave a scornful sigh: "That's all I'd need."

She yawned. You could feel her relaxing into oblivion. I put my arm around her. "I didn't get much sleep last night either." She slumped into me.

"Watch out, I may drop off in your arms."

Instead we grabbed for each other, bringing lips and thighs and fingers together. "God, you smell good," she murmured. "Like leather harnesses or something."

"Flattering the old horse?"

"You need a shave, horse."

"I had a hard night."

"Come in and have a drink with me."

Across the lawn the side door of the house threw a slice of light into the drive. Then the door chunked shut. Carol nuzzled: "Where's that zipper?"

"Looks like Mehdi's going out on a house call."

"Let's go home and cuddle."

"Got to go to work." I kissed her. She tried to hang on to my hand, so in pulling away I gave her a fuller kiss.

"Wait."

"No time."

"I'll be home."

By the time I got to my Volvo, Mehdi's Mercedes was already halfway to Storrow Drive, but I had an idea where he might be headed.

Larry must have been waiting up for him.

Outside the ugly little apartment building the Mercedes was parked blocking a driveway. Its vanity plate read "MEHDI." Down the block under a streetlight I looked over the meager tool kit in the Volvo's trunk. Not very encouraging. Someday Santa Claus will bring me a shotgun mike, transmitter bugs, and a few other prosthetic devices. In the meantime I was sorry to be missing the conversation in Larry's living room.

Rather than mope about it, I turned my attention to the casement window in Larry's bedroom. It was barely open enough to permit a screwdriver and hex key to unhitch the operator arm so the frame could swing free. I stood on the banana seat of a kid's bike and worked fast. Unlike conventional metal screens, which cut with a loud snoring sound, fiberglass screens respond well to a sharp pocketknife.

From inside Larry's bedroom I could hear them negotiating. From the kitchen I could see the living-room sofa reflected in the mirror on the wall behind the television. Mehdi had Duke across his lap and was fondling the pointy bulldog ears.

"Because he's an asshole," Larry's voice insisted.

"You already said that."

"Well, it's true."

"If he's such a fool, why did you talk to him?"

"I had to. He was threatening me."

"What can he do to you?"

"He knows about my plants."

Mehdi sniffed: "They don't shoot you for that."

"Look," Larry growled. "You steal millions in stocks or whatnot and maybe you pay a fine. You cultivate a taboo weed, it means your job. Maybe prison."

"Get rid of the plants."

"How could I? He was right there in my kitchen threatening to call the cops. And why should I have to terminate them?" Larry began to spit and pop: "I mean, Jesus Christ, this is your problem not mine. All I did was do Jerry a favor. I didn't gain anything by it. Why should I have to—"

"You want some profit for yourself. No problem."

"Bullshit," Larry squawked. "All I want is to be unplugged from this circuit when it blows." He was pacing in and out of my line of sight. He'd traded the sweatpants for powder-blue jeans and a plaid cowboy shirt. "Maybe Ames is a federal asshole. At work we have agency spies up the ass. Everybody's paranoid."

"Let me explain to you." Mehdi prepared to massage Lawrence T. Lillo's brain. "The police will be asking everything about Jerry Schell. For a few days, maybe a few weeks."

"I'll deny it," Larry sputtered. "I can deny the whole—"

"No, no. The important thing is, in Jerry's bedroom closet the police found the gun that killed Mrs. O'Hare."

"You're kidding me."

"Ames told me."

"That gives me the creeps."

In the mirror Mehdi sat stroking the bulldog. His geniality had a raw edge now: "You don't talk to Ames, okay?"

"I'll use my own judgment."

"No, you say nothing. Very simple."

"Don't order me around," Larry protested.

Mehdi stood up, putting Duke on the floor: "You say nothing to Ames. Okay?"

He spoke with a sort of diplomatic precision, moving to the door. The bulldog whimpered. Suddenly Larry choked with alarm: "Hey, what's going on? What the—"

The bulldog began a panting squeal of pain. I watched him drag his hind end across the green shag rug. He was paralyzed. Mehdi turned: "Your baby has a problem."

Larry dropped to his knees: "What did you do to him?"

When Larry touched the dog, Duke let out a roar like a pig in a slaughterhouse. His tail twitched, his hind legs seemed completely lifeless. He dragged his dead hindquarters past Larry's workout bench, giving off rapid little howls. Larry lurched to his feet in a rage:

"You—"

He piled into Mehdi and slammed him into the door.

The dog headed behind the sofa, his tail feebly twitching. Larry ducked sideways. From the workout bench he snatched up one of his dumbbells and waved it in Mehdi's face like a war club, on the verge of low-tech homicide. Mehdi said calmly, "You need help with your dog?"

"What did you do to him?"

"Maybe he gets old."

"He's a goddamn puppy. He's won ribbons, he's worth five hundred bucks."

"Too bad."

"You broke his back," Larry roared. "You broke his fucking back."

"You want help? Move." Mehdi brushed Larry aside. He scooped up the animal and went back to the sofa. With Duke in his lap facing away from him, his thumbs probed along the spine. "I help you," he said to nobody in particular, "and you help me. Yes?"

The dog yelped. Larry swore.

"Yes?"

"Okay," Larry snarled. "Hurry up."

Whatever Mehdi did or undid, his slow-motion karate worked. This time when he put the bulldog down, Duke waddled to his master as if the healer had said, "Pick up thy bed and walk, ye dog of little faith!"

Mehdi left, brushing doggy hairs off his pants.

I was halfway across the kitchen when Duke suddenly remembered he was a dog and sensed me in the house. He tore across the vinyl floor, toenails clicking, and skidded into me, yapping fortissimo. I discouraged him with my shoe, but by then Larry was in the kitchen trying to squeeze my Adam's apple out my left nostril. "Let go," I choked. "You're making—"

He was raving at me.

Technically Larry was right. I shouldn't have been there. On the other hand, your Adam's apple will not pass through your nostril without considerable discomfort. When I couldn't pry his hands off my neck and I felt cartilage crunching, a blast of adrenaline hit me. I put my fist in Larry's groin and, while his mind was occupied, pushed him back onto the kitchen table. He twisted over onto his side. "Don't," he croaked.

Duke sat on his ass and yipped now and then. I could barely move my neck. To Larry Lillo I said, "Your friend's in trouble. I wouldn't go near him while he's under surveillance. If I were you."

Larry lay there in fetal position murmuring. I took a twenty from my wallet.

"This is for the screen in your bedroom. You'll want to tighten it up, mosquito season's coming."

At this point it didn't make sense to exit through the window, stepping on a ridiculous bicycle, so I followed Mehdi out the front door.

Chapter Thirty

Carol's face was full of sleep. I hung back in the apartment doorway.

"I shouldn't have woken you."

"Come in," she murmured. "I wasn't sleeping very well."

She poured me a wallop of Bushmill's Irish and put on the kettle for herself. I opened the drapes and we nestled together on the sofa in the dark living room. The hall light cut the room in two. The night sky ouside could have been the crushing darkness at the bottom of the sea.

"The cops found a pistol in Jerry's apartment," I said. "It looks like the item used on your mother."

"You told me."

"I just overheard Mehdi Farhat telling Larry Lillo the news. And he was using details—where the pistol was found—that he couldn't have known unless he'd seen it there. Or put it there himself."

"Mehdi?"

"He's talking as if he and Jerry were doing business together."

"Was Jerry doing legal work for him?"

"My guess is, they've been looting an estate that Jerry's

settling. Mehdi's health palace in Norwood is going up on land finagled from the estate. And your mother was in on it."

"Oh great."

"Maybe Jerry was using the others to do his grabbing for him."

"Which might account for the payments he made to Mehdi?"

"Could." The kettle began to hiss in the kitchenette. "It could also explain what went wrong in the lovers' triangle."

"Such as?"

"An hour before Dorothy died your aunt heard Jerry bawling her out for being greedy. Maybe Dorothy was blackmailing both Jerry and her boss."

"Do we have any proof?"

"Monday morning I'll look up Mehdi's land in Norwood at the Registry of Deeds. To see if Jerry was feeding him chunks of the Carter estate."

Carol half groaned, half sighed: "Does it matter? They can't disbar him now. Even if Jerry killed my mother, nobody can do anything about it now." The kettle hissed fiercely. Carol sagged against my shoulder: "I suppose guilt must have been one of the things pushing him into the drug overdose last night. I don't care what anybody thinks, Jerry was basically a very decent guy."

I went into the kitchen and spilled some coffee beans into the grinder. While it snarled them to powder, I set up a filter and tried to think. Carol's favorite mug sported a cartoon in which a cat in a surgical mask was sewing nine cats together. Under the nine wildly surprised faces the caption read: "A stitch in nine saves time."

Carol took the mug and made room for me again on the sofa.

"One mystery," I said, "is how Mehdi Farhat knew that a pistol was in Jerry's closet."

"You think—?" Carol gave a soft, nauseated groan.

"It's possible Mehdi had as much reason to silence your mother as Jerry did."

"But someone shot at his house the other night."

"My first thought was Jerry. Unless Mehdi did it himself to deflect suspicion."

"Oh come on. You mean Mehdi's sending these American Satan threats himself?"

"Or being a copycat."

"That's a lot of ifs."

"True. But there's a lot at stake."

Carol tipped some of my Irish whiskey into her hot coffee. "Duncan, are we imagining things?"

"You can find out."

"Me?" Her voice flinched.

"Mehdi wanted you at his party tonight."

"So I ask him for another cocktail hotdog please, and oh, by the way, did you murder my mother the other night?"

"He put up money to send you to Tufts. He admires you. His daughter needs you. He needs you."

"God, even your best friend you don't tell about murder."

"But you might tell someone who loved you. Who's confessed—with great pain and shyness of course—that she hated her mother too."

"You mean make a play for him? Me? You're crazy."

"You told me yourself that he's been sweet on you for a long time."

"Hey, whoa. I said my *mother* had some wild idea that he—"

"He's known you for years. Given you presents. Including this gorgeous rug. The point is, he's attracted to you. And you're not a married woman now. You're old friends, you need someone in your life."

"Not *him*."

"Sari tells me she daydreams about the two of you getting married. She senses something in dad. Count on it."

"Oh no. No way." Fear, disgust, and temptation mixed in her voice. She was wide awake now. "I couldn't do it, Duncan. If you're wrong about him, the guilt would kill me."

"Why? In that case you'd be proving his innocence without any damaging scandal. No cops. And he'd never be the wiser."

She ignored this. "And if you're right, I wouldn't know how to act. He'd see right through me. I'd be a babbling idiot, and he'd kill me."

"You wouldn't be such a pushover."

"The idea's crazy."

"But it will work."

"You're insinuating he's killed people." She got to her feet, clapping her palms to her jaw. "If he touched me I'd die."

I shook my head: "You'd tell him you love him. You've never loved anyone this way. You feel the wind knocked out of you. It kills you to be away from him. It's a tremendous relief to confess that to him after all these months. Years."

"What about Carol the married woman?"

"You've always been fascinated by him, from the moment he first touched your arm as a kid, a teenage girl still missing her father."

"Oh my God."

"When he treated you a few years ago, you were amazed at the feelings that took hold of you again. The pleasure, the happiness. You wanted to grab his hands and guide him to touch you. You almost offered him a massage, just to feel the heat of his body in your hands."

"Have you ever noticed his little potbelly?"

"But you respected him too much. You know he grew up in a society where women have to show special restraint and care. You knew about his ruined marriage, you sensed his pain." I took another swallow of Bushmill's Irish painkiller. "Also you were terrified of your mother's resentment. Her jealousy."

"Her protectiveness."

"Right. Her monopoly on both of you. And now that your mother's gone, you can follow your heart. You've dreamed about living in that fantastic house, skipping off to Kenya with him, or the Riviera, wherever he fancies. Now you can let him draw you close. You can be a mother to Sari, let her push you and her father together. And Sari's no fool, she sensed the cruel streak in Dorothy too. The hateful streak you experienced all your life. Including Dorothy's determination to force you into a marriage you didn't want—for the money, the prestige, fill in the blanks. Only to turn against Jerry when he failed to produce the goods. The last straw."

"That's not all made up."

"So much the better. You're both underdogs finally getting a grip on life. Both divorced. Both doctors."

"I wouldn't mind opening a pediatric clinic in his new medical complex. Help plan the thing."

"Of course. It's natural. You'll need to know who's putting up the money. After all, Jerry told you things, your mother did. Mehdi can clear up the details for you."

"Duncan, it's so cold-blooded."

"Look. All you have to do is be around him. Go out with him. See Sari as usual. Unless I miss my guess, Mehdi will do the rest. Just let the old relationship evolve into something a little deeper, that's all."

A 747 from Logan passed over us with the roar of a heavenly vacuum cleaner, leaving raw silence. "Duncan," she said softly. "I'm scared."

"Once you're face-to-face with that smile of his, holding hands, it'll feel perfectly natural. How long have you known him?"

"I'm not in any shape to think this through."

"Take your time. Maybe we can get you a date for tomorrow night."

"Very funny."

"No joke. In the morning you call to apologize for missing the party. You wonder how Sari's doing, you miss her. Maybe the two of you could take Sari to the aquarium this afternoon, or the Children's Museum."

"It could prove he's innocent. As you said."

"Sure." After the display of cruelty I'd just witnessed in Larry's living room I had my doubts, but why discourage Carol?

"I've got to put my head down," she said. "I'm whipped."

Lying in bed at my side, silent, she faced the wall, away from me, the robe wrapped tight. She reached up to shut off the frilly lamp on the night table, then backed her bottom firmly into me with a series of little wiggles, like a cat about to pounce. I was wondering how to challenge the gloom in the air. After a while Carol seemed to read my mind. At least she took my hand and slipped it into the robe, hugging the hand that hugged her breast. Her voice sounded wonderfully sleepy: "I feel like I'm floating on the ocean. Rocking on the ocean. Very gently. In a boat. A snug sailboat. That won't ever sink."

"Am I with you?"

"Mmm. You're the boat, silly." We drifted on the current for a moment, then she added, "Didn't you daydream about boats when you were little?"

"Tugboats, maybe. Clipper ships. Battleships."

"Typical little boy."

"I'm afraid. Or fire engines. I was a fire-engine nut."

"Right now you're a dear, strong sailboat cradling me in the ocean. All sunny and warm and peaceful. For a few minutes at least."

"As long as you want."

"Just hold me safe like this, very gentle." It was an easy wish to fill. She was rocking softly against me and I began to pick up the rhythm. "Tomorrow morning," she murmured, "I have to get up and be responsible again. But for this minute I'm just me, feeling very . . ."

"Mmm?"

"Very amazingly safe and . . . and appreciated."

"Loved."

"Mmm." The current rocked us along blissfully. In the dark I squeezed her tightly in my arms, not wanting the surge of feeling to end. I said, "It's been a long time since I've felt this way."

"That makes me happy." She rolled over now to search my face in the gloom. "Duncan, if we were in bed together—just in theory—are we the kind of people . . . I mean, at the end of a terrible day, would we be able to talk out all our little job horrors with each other? I mean, could we give each other some peace? Or would we just drive each other nuts?"

As I was assuring her what a peace-loving guy I am, the phone by the bed rang. We both jumped. The digital clock said 2:30. Carol picked up the receiver, then handed it to me.

"God," Rachel cried. "I've been phoning everywhere. Where have you been?"

"I told you I'd be late. Don't wait up."

"Where have you been!" she scolded. "Somebody broke the living-room window with a bullet."

For a moment I felt the ugly fact beating in my head. I asked Rachel, "You okay?"

"Just flipped out, that's all. The police came. They're having a cruiser go by the house every so often tonight."

A cold blade of guilt went up under my ribs. "What time did it happen?"

"Just before midnight."

"Were you in the room when the shot was fired?"

"We were watching the tube. Waiting for you."

"What part of the window was hit? High or low?"

"High. The bullet made a hole up by the ceiling. Mom will have a bird."

"Better up high than down where you live."

"That's what I told Sean."

"Sit tight and I'll see you in twenty."

Instead of hanging up she came back at me: "I had a feeling you might be there. What's going on?"

"I'm working."

"This is unbelievable. If I get shot while my father is out fooling around, oh wow." Her voice shivered with disgust.

"See you in twenty minutes." I hung up, kissed Carol, and began buttoning my shirt. "Somebody's fired at the house again. This time through the front window."

"That's awful."

"Awful marksmanship." I groped for my shoes under the bed. "Get some sleep. I'll see you tomorrow. Call your host with regrets for missing the party. Shoot for the aquarium."

I bent down for a touch of sweet sorrow, then headed for the door.

"Wait!" She leaned up on her elbow with a mixture of dismay and relief in her face: "The broken window. When did it happen?"

"Just before midnight."

"Then it couldn't have been Mehdi. Could it."

"I was with him at midnight."

"Who then?"

I shrugged: "The American Satan."

Rachel gave me a welcome hug, and then in a delayed reaction to the night's terrors she started shivering in my arms. "I put out the lights right away, like you said, and tried to get a look at the car. But it was kind of hit-and-run."

"Like last time."

"Sean wanted me to sleep at his house, but I thought I'd better be home when you called."

"You've got courage, kid."

The living-room window was neatly starred in the upper left-hand corner. No question, someone was trying to communicate with me.

I took a shower, ate a succulent pink grapefruit and some shredded wheat, and then rolled into bed. In my mind's eye I saw hands cracking bulldog spines one after another like diners tearing apart steamed clams. My back began to ache.

Then Rachel was in the doorway, barefoot but still in her jeans and sweatshirt. The hall light glistened in her hair. "Hey," she murmured. "I can't sleep."

She came over and stretched out on the bed, on what used to be my side. The mattress registered the weight of an adult body, and I tried to picture the pip-squeak who used to squirrel in between Meg and me, all elbows and pointy knees, with monsters in hot pursuit.

"When I saw that hole in the window," she said, "I thought, *I could even die*. One weirdo, one stupid accident, that's all. Blip. I mean, what if the atomic-power plant down in Plymouth blew up, or a car smashed into you, like Mom—I mean, a priest, a *priest* for God's sake, who would've expected a priest? It's like the world is ready to kill you anytime it—"

"You didn't know that?"

"I sort of did and I didn't. You know?"

Her voice hovered in the darkness, disembodied, not young or old. It was the deeper, private voice I'd heard snatches of since she'd been a toddler—not the bossy rebel, full of magical overconfidence, but the unfooled four-year-old who looked me in the eye and stammered: "I don't want to go to heaven, you can't do anything there."

I gave her arm a squeeze. She leaned down across my chest so my arm would reach around her waist. Her breath smelled of potato chips.

"In case you're wondering," I said, "every day's a miracle of survival. And I'm really not sure what it all means either. But basically I'm in favor of it."

"It makes me think, since we may all be dead, maybe me and Sean, maybe we should just go and get married or something."

The soft warmth of a woman's breast pressed against

my shirt. I felt an ache in my ribs thinking of the temptation to keep playing kid to postpone life's fatal choices. In the silence the refrigerator cycled on in the kitchen. "When I came back from Vietnam," I said, "sudden marriage looked like the answer to me too."

"Did it work?"

"That used to be my side of the bed you're on."

"Did you love her?"

"Head over heels. But you can't hide out in other people. You still have to go to work Monday mornings and change the kids' smelly diapers."

"I'm not ready for that. I graduate next year and I've hated every dumb job I've had. And babies really scare me. Where would we live? These days you'd have to work a hundred years to buy the crummiest dump on this street."

"Times have been tougher."

"That's easy for you to say."

"Look, I know you. You have brains, you can do damn near anything. It's all a matter of finding something you love."

"That's easy for you. You're a guy. And you've got this rich doctor you're in love with."

"Carol's not rich."

"Is she as sexy as she tries to look? She's got a great body. Except her calves are too thin."

"I'm interested in her mind."

"Oh, sure."

"Aren't you sleepy? It must be after three."

"Yeah, well." She was lying on her back. I had a feeling her eyes were open in the dark. Then I felt her reaching over to muss my hair, her thumb clumsily catching in my ear. She rubbed my head for a few minutes like a lucky rabbit's foot. Out back the neighbor's beagle complained to the god of beagles about the darkness in his soul, then fell back to sleep. I was just about gone when Rachel said: "Got your pistol here?"

"On the night table."

"Loaded?"

"Come on. Go to sleep."

"If it's okay with you," she croaked under her breath, "I'll just lie here for a while and think. Okay?"

Chapter Thirty-One

"We're going to the aquarium this afternoon," Carol rattled over the phone. "He may ask me to dinner afterward."

"Lucky you."

"I'll be too scared to swallow."

"When you know him better," I suggested, "I'll rig up a little tape recorder for your purse."

"And in the meantime," she said acidly, "what am I supposed to be doing?"

"Winning his confidence."

"Great. If I get any shakier I'll pee my pants."

At two-thirty I parked across the street from Carol's building. Through my binoculars they made a fine family: Dashing Dad in his white turtleneck and blazer, the acting Mom in an apricot dress more feminine than any hospital duds. Bouncy Daughter wore a white jersey with a flotilla of red and blue sailboats on it. The vanity plate simplified tailing Dad's buggy, though they had only a few blocks to drive.

At the aquarium they kept together at first, Daughter self-consciously strolling between Mom and Dad, giving each a hand, deliberately bringing them together and putting herself in the picture. With her brother back in prep school she had the adults to herself. After Sari grew restless and began wandering off on her own, Mehdi stayed close to Carol. From time to time as they passed the thick glass tanks, he would guide her to an interesting specimen with a touch on the arm, a confidential murmur in the willing ear. Even at this distance the crease in his trousers looked sharp.

In the eddying crowds Carol let herself float closer and closer to him. She laughed with him, rewarding his quips with a pat on his blazer sleeve and eyes sparkling with praise.

Peering through the portholes in the side of the big central fish tank, Carol and Sari ogled the creatures soaring in the shadowy water above them—shark and ray and a delicate balletic turtle—while boys on the platform at the top threw pennies that sank past the animals like the gods' trash. Sari and Carol made faces at the fish.

At one point Carol spotted me in the sea of bodies behind her and gave me a dirty look, but I couldn't be sure. Perhaps we would never trust each other again. The thought hurt.

Afterward the family took a stroll around Fanueil Hall and Quincy Market, where Daughter got Dad to buy her a maple cutting board in the shape of a sperm whale, which she proceeded to use on his backside like a fraternity pledge paddle until the joke got to him. Nobody could have looked less like a murderer.

I had a couple slices of pizza while they dined behind the swanky fake-Tudor windows of the Four-Loaf Cleaver up the street from the Union Oyster House. Then it was home to the manse in Brookline, Mom on Dad's arm.

Just after midnight Rachel was humiliating Sean and me at Scrabble—she'd just assembled *quizzical*—when the phone rang. Rachel gave Sean a Significant Look.

"I'm back," Carol said.

"Learn anything?"

"He's very sweet. He thought the octopus looked like his bald-headed uncle in Iran. He bought Sari a wooden whale for her wall. She was glad to get out of the house. We were gawking at the toadfish or some ugly thing, and she blurted, 'Look at that face. He needs to get made over in the hospital.' I almost died."

"What about the Iranian shark?"

"Mehdi was seeing patients the night of the murder."

"You asked him outright?"

"I pretended I'd tried to phone him. His office appointment book should say if he was really there."

"We'll have a look. What did he say about your mother?"

"Nothing. That he missed her help. That he could still feel my sorrow. Quote unquote."

"You let him peek into your melancholy heart?"

"I used your line about what a witch she'd been to me."

"Did he take the bait?"

"It ended up with him defending her and me sounding like an ungrateful brat. Dorothy was stubborn, was all he'd say. And that you have to be stubborn in business. Oh, and she was handling the leases in his new medical complex for him. He asked if I knew any specialists who might want to relocate."

"And?"

"I told him I was considering opening up a pediatric practice myself. Not real subtle."

"Did he bite?"

"Just as you predicted. He loved the idea. It would fulfill a dream for my mother. And him too. He quizzed me about it at dinner. We ate at the Four-Loaf Cleaver—they're doing nouvelle cuisine now, very light. I was a total pig."

"Is he looking for doctors who don't mind working with chiropractors?"

"It's hard setting up a practice. So Mehdi's offering goodies like computer record-keeping and help in hiring a receptionist and the works. And there's nothing really shady about chiropractors."

"How do you feel about his claims to relieve retardation by squeezing kids' skulls?"

"He actually says that?"

"It's in one of his ads. He's certified by some institute to squeeze heads."

"Don't tell me. I've got to believe in this guy if I'm going to go through with this."

"When do you see him again?"

"Monday night. After my shift."

"Good."

"I like him, Duncan. He can be such a nice guy. I've always like being around him."

"We need his office keys."

She caught her breath: "You don't want much, do you?"

"It's important."

She groaned.

"You can copy a key in a minute. I'll show you."

"I may have my hands full Monday night."

"All you have to—" Then I realized what she meant. "So. Things have already come a long way then. Good."

"And you," she teased bitterly, "you're not even jealous."

CHAPTER THIRTY-TWO

Sunday afternoon on McDermott Street in Hyde Park kids were playing street hockey with a tennis ball and kamikaze sincerity. The houses were high and narrow, as if holding their breath. Some had vinyl siding that skinned over their architectural trim and made windows look naked as eyes with shaved eyebrows and no lashes. The Clancys lived behind striped aluminum awnings, enclosed by a waist-high fence with green and white aluminum strips running on the diagonal. Mr. C was flying Old Glory in the front yard and scrubbing his Buick in the driveway. The "Sexy Senior Citizen" sign still winked in the back window. I let him go into his backyard for the hose before I presented myself at the front door.

Through the screen I could hear Gladys Clancy playing "Ain't Misbehavin' " on an electric organ that keened like a sawmill. Gladys remembered me from the funeral and put me in a frilly easy chair in her living room. We confessed our mutual love of Fats Waller. "Here," she said changing her glasses, "let me put on my normal lenses."

At one end of the room a jumbo television squatted on a pine cobbler's bench. On the organ were a bowling trophy, a cute china bell, and photos of graduating sons.

On the wall Jesus was hanging in there, and in a gilt frame Mr. Clancy and another dolled-up Legionnaire were shaking hands. Gladys beamed:

"George is washing the car."

"Good day for it."

"Shall I call him in?"

"Let him wash. I won't be long."

"Can I offer you some peanut brittle?"

"I wanted to ask you about the real-estate deal your sister offered you."

"Oh that." Gladys sat down in a tall rocker with frilly pads bow-tied to the seat and back. "I was never really tempted. Dorothy was always one for the big ideas. And toward the end there she was more frantic than ever. Not well, if you want my opinion. I didn't like her color. I told Carol different times, 'I don't like your mother's color.' "

"Who was the seller of the properties, do you remember?"

"Oh heavens, I don't know. Some estate or trust or other."

"Was Dorothy's employer a party to the sale?"

"Dr. Farhat? Oh, he was in on it somehow, but I'm kind of vague on it now. Dottie's idea was, buy low and sell high."

"You sound dubious."

"No no," she protested. "It's the truth. I swear."

"Doubtful, I mean. You sound doubtful."

"Well who wouldn't be? After Dottie lost the bank money they'd borrowed for Carol's medical college, that did it for me. Sister or no sister. Carol went to Tufts, you know."

"How much did Dottie lose?"

"Whatever two years costs. Thousands."

"How'd she lose it?"

"Oh well now, she bought a bunch of worthless bonds. It was supposed to be buy low and sell high all over again. Beat the bank interest on the loan."

"That was when Jerry Schell came along?"

"That's right. See, she didn't want Carol marrying him since he wasn't of her faith. But he had money, see, and I think Dottie hoped he could get back the money for her. And when he couldn't, oh, was she ever down on him."

"And the loss hadn't been his fault."

"Not a bit of it. Oh no, she wanted someone to blame. She used to pull that trick when we were small."

"Carol must've been upset."

"Mr. Ames, if we'd of been a fly on the wall, I hate to think. Of course Carol's too good a daughter to complain to us. And the chiropractor, Dr. Farhat, made up the money. As a bonus, I was told. For helping him find some big deal. If you can believe that."

Perhaps Dorothy had earned her bonus by introducing Mehdi to Jerry Schell. Gladys went on, mostly rubbing old wounds. So I changed the subject: "What was Dorothy's husband like?"

"Eddie? Oh he was a good scout. We used to play cards with them lots of nights when my mother was still alive. My sister was a great one for cards. Took after my mother."

"What kind of work did Eddie do?"

"Eddie took over his family's appliance store over by Franklin Park. Sales and service, he did. But small, you see, so it was hard to keep up with these big discount outfits that slash the prices. What do they care? I mean, it's fine if nothing ever breaks down on you, but—"

"He took his own life, Carol says."

"Franklin Park's all colored now."

Gladys sat motionless in the rocker, hands in her lap, her sparkle-edged eyeglasses tilted slightly on her broad face. I nudged her: "Was he bankrupt?"

"Eddie was caught in the middle, between the big discount places and the coloreds taking over there. In ten years that neighborhood went from beautiful to the dumps. The stores that didn't get robbed got burned and boarded up. Nobody was left who could buy anything. It's no secret how the colored spend their money. Eddie was held up once with a sword like they cut sugarcane with—"

"A machete."

"Mmm, one of those. That's why he had the gun there in the first place."

"What gun?"

"He had to buy a pistol. For the store. But he got to taking it home with him after work, especially if he had a dollar on him. And that was what he used."

"Shot himself."

"Nobody suspected he was so discouraged, except maybe Dottie. She kept the books, you see. But she'd never admit anything was wrong. Poor Carol suffered the worst of it."

"I didn't know."

"Oh, she doesn't talk about it." Gladys was enjoying her command over these ancient taboos. When I solemnly begged for the details, as she wanted me to, she drew a dramatic preliminary breath. "Well." She nipped a speck of peanut brittle and nibbled invisibly. Then: "Eddie picked an ordinary Sunday. We'd seen them only the night before, for cards. You'd never of suspected a thing. He was going to be an authorized Whirlpool dealer. It was all set up. So Dorothy went out to Sunday Mass and was gone all day, heaven knows where—she was never home when Carol was growing up. Visiting this one or that."

"Carol was home alone with her father?"

"Oh yes. They got along fine."

"Oh."

"And no sooner was Dorothy out of the house than Eddie went upstairs into the attic cubbyhole—it was a hatch affair in the upstairs hall ceiling—and he pulled up the ladder behind him. On springs, it was."

"And Carol heard the shot."

"That's right. She'd had a battle with her mother about not going to Mass. She was eating Sugar Corn Pops and the gun went off, faraway sounding. And she couldn't find her father anywhere. So she went back downstairs and looked at TV and felt strange. Then after about an hour she went through the house calling his name, and on up the stairs too, where she saw the stains on the hall carpet and heard the drip. So she got a chair, and when she opened the hatch his head started to come down too the way he was lying, so she got a towel and wrapped it around his head as best she could. Then she closed the hatch up again."

"She didn't call anyone?"

"That's the awful part. She knew there was nothing anybody could do. And she knew he wouldn't want people looking at him, certainly not police. So she went back downstairs and waited out the day lying on the sofa without a peep, till after dark, when her mother came home."

"God. The poor kid."

"Dorothy just about had a breakdown. She was a basket case. They stayed with us about a week. I was glad to do what I could."

"What about Carol?"

"It was right after that they began to talk about her being a doctor. See, she must've been lying in that house all day long wishing for some magic doctor to bring her father back."

"No wonder she doesn't talk about it."

"I can show you a picture of Eddie if you want." She was already on her feet. From a wicker magazine rack by the organ she picked out a thick photo album. The images moved over the years from black-and-white to faded colors and, most recently, true tones. Arrow-shaped black paste-ins tacked down each snapshot's corners. "Here it is. Carol was about seven."

It was a flash shot, full of flare and glare. A man and a girl stood in front of a white-jacketed coal furnace in a dim cellar. The man stood behind the girl, stooping, as if hugging her. He was short and balding, with a fringe of curly reddish hair. He wore chino work pants and, under a nebbishy bump of a nose, a good-natured grin. The girl had on red corduroy overalls. Her reddish hair was drawn back in third-grader pigtails, her face crushed into ferocious concentration as she squinted down the barrel of the pistol the man was helping her hold. His meaty hands enclosed her hands, aiming—my heart tripped—a long black Ruger target pistol identical to the weapon in Jerry Schell's apartment.

After I left Gladys, I went into the hospital to see Meg, thinking I might strike up a conversation about heirloom pistols with a passing doctor. As it turned out, Meg had visitors, girlfriends from work plus a widowed electrician she'd dated a few times. She'd shed most of her bandages above the neck and Rachel had helped her with some makeup. She looked pretty happy.

Dr. Schell had already made her rounds and wasn't expected back. According to Rachel, Meg had a crush on the electrician, so I didn't make a pest of myself.

Chapter Thirty-Three

On Monday, Jerry Schell's law partners were shy about going over the status of the Carter estate with me. After a morning of tender solicitations I gave up and went out to the Norfolk County Registry of Deeds in Dedham, where I found that on the day I'd met Dorothy O'Hare, Sunrise Associates had signed on the dotted line for a hundred acres of land with frontage on Route 1 in Norwood. First among the associates, in a boyish scrawl that leaped every which way, came Mehdi Farhat, D.C.

Next door in Probate, I looked up Olive Carter's will. The several heirs roosted on the West Coast. I logged them into my notebook for future reference.

When I drove out to Mehdi's hundred acres I found a locked construction trailer and a lone bulldozer grading the site. The bulldozer was skinning grass off one of the last open stretches along Route 1, between a shopping center and a car dealership: a spot destined for lucrative development.

A sign twice my height decreed Spirit Plaza. In gold letters a smaller sign prescribed the health complex, listing three chiropractors, two M.D.s, a homeopath, a physical-therapy group, a gym, health-food and sporting-goods stores, and one death-defying New Age touchy-feelie enterprise, the Wholistic Rebirthing Center. While the bulldozer gouged the stony ground and the May wildflowers twitched in the breeze, I gawked at the signs, trying to imagine how any of this could be a spur to murder.

Carol's phone didn't answer.

At ten o'clock I reluctantly left Rachel locked up in the house doing algebra homework and headed into Boston. Carol's BMW sat in Mehdi's moonlit driveway. I waited down the street while on Old Time Radio the Lone Ranger shot up the Volvo with silver bullets.

Sometime after midnight the BMW shot past me. By the time I caught up with its taillights the car was in the underground garage and Carol was waiting for the elevator. I called to her through the steel gate that closed the garage entrance. She turned, the neon light giving her face a bloodless pallor: "Duncan? Is that you? You scared me."

"I've been trying to reach you all day."

She came up the ramp to let me in. "I put in a long, long shift yesterday. So this afternoon I switched off the phone to sleep. And forgot it."

"You saw Mehdi tonight."

"Mmm. Things are getting complicated."

"You're lovers."

"Getting there."

"Ah hell."

"You were the one urging me on," she grumbled. She stuck her security card into the slot and the steel gate rose with a grinding whir. I took her hand.

Inside the elevator Carol bumped me softly with her hip. "Move over a bit." Then she turned to punch the control panel. "How did you know I let Mehdi make love to me?"

"For one thing, your hair looks like a tag-team match."

"All I had to do was lie there and twitch now and then. Like a good Catholic girl."

"Sorry to hear it."

"I have to enjoy it?"

"Christ," I muttered, "don't make it more painful than it is. I was hoping you'd get close to him before you ended up in the sack together."

"I tried to tell you the other night. This is the twentieth century. The real world. But you wouldn't listen. It was such a great idea. Want me to call him and break it off once and for all? Well? You see what I meant?"

I nodded: "It hurts."

In the silence she leaned back against the elevator's fake wood paneling. A slow, wide, silly smile came over her face, interrupted by the soft jolt of arrival. The corridor had a stale synthetic smell. Once in the apartment Carol stepped out of her shoes and flipped on the bright living-room lamp. The red rug blazed to life, and on the wall the African mask winked at me. Carol said, "I have to go back to the basement to do some wash. I have nothing to wear."

"You look your best in nothing."

"Don't be naughty. Here, have some wine while you wait." While Carol fetched the laundry bag and a bottle of the tangy Muller-Thurgau she liked, I dialed Rachel, who mumbled, "How can I sleep with you bothering me like this? Let me sleep, okay?"

"Go for it."

"Wait. You be home for breakfast?"

"Of course."

"Don't let me forget my gym stuff. She'll kill me."

"Sweet dreams."

"Sweet dreams, old man."

The receiver clicked and I felt a twinge of something like regret. Shouldering the striped laundry bag, Carol said, "You have a nice relationship with Rachel."

"It's getting better. Not much happens on the surface."

"It never much does." She headed for the door. I grabbed the bottle of wine.

"I'll keep you company."

The humming elevator could have been in the hospital, going to an underground operating room. In fact the laundry room was a concrete bunker lined with coin-op machines. Carol stuffed in her laundry and hit me up for quarters to run it. There were a few plastic chairs but we stayed on our feet doggedly eye-to-eye. I filled the glasses. The Muller-Thurgau was tart, and the smell of bleach in the air gave it a sour bite.

"So"—she sipped—"who goes first?"

"One thing's definite," I said. "Jerry grabbed the land for Mehdi's health complex from the Carter estate. A steal."

"Somebody must have approved the sale."

"I phoned one of the heirs in Seattle. She claims that last year the state DEQE ruled—"

"The what?"

"Department of Environmental Quality. Back in November they defined the Norwood acreage as wetlands, with building restrictions that knocked the real-estate appraisal way down."

"Mehdi's defying them?"

"No need. By a nice coincidence DEQE has revised its judgment. Suddenly only a few acres are wetland. The rest is choice real estate."

"So Mehdi had an inside tip."

"Or left a tip for services rendered."

"A bribe."

"My bet is, Morris Field is behind the appraisal and took home a gratuity."

"Mehdi told me Jerry made the heirs a low offer to save them fees and commissions and speed up the sale."

"I steal your shoes so you won't trip over the laces."

"Can you see anybody going to jail over it?" She raised her glass and guzzled a bit. "God, this is depressing."

"That's my story," I said. "What about yours?"

"Mine?" The washing machine rumbled and churned, sloshing sudsy clothes against the glass door. "Oh my God," she croaked. "I just gave myself a scare. For a second I thought I saw a baby inside there, flopping around in the dirty water."

"One of your kids missing?"

"Very funny."

"You're stalling. What happened tonight?"

"Nothing. We ate. We talked. We let Sari shoot us with a toy gun. We screwed."

"Let's not fool around."

"Oh let's." She gave me a mock-seductive grin which faded fast. "What can I tell you?" she demanded irritably. "The other night we were talking about Africa, so tonight Mehdi hired some Ethiopian lady to prepare a real Ethiopian meal in his kitchen, these large wheels of bread, like a sourdough pizza crust, with scoops of spicy—"

"Carol—"

"Get off my back," she snapped. "I'm only doing this nasty little trick for you."

"You find out where Mehdi keeps his keys?"

I thought she might kick me. "You're warped, Duncan. You really are. Why do I even talk to you? I mean, here you are planning to break into the man's house, you have me spying on him, breathing all kinds of lies in his ear, lulling him to sleep in my arms like a baby. Oh Jesus. I must be crazy."

"You've had a very emotional evening."

"Oh have I?" She threw the words back mincingly: "A *very* emotional evening. Mr. Smartass. Mr. Conceited Smartass. Do your own shitty tricks."

"You found out something."

"Go to hell."

"Carol—"

"Look. It's nothing big. There are two recent *Wall Street Journal*s in the rack under the TV. So he reads it sometimes. Him and ninety million other people."

"Exactly what happened tonight?"

"Oh stuff it."

"You got closer to Mehdi than you expected."

"Nothing happened. We talked medicine and I unloaded on him. About what a factory the hospital can be. We lost a young girl last winter just because of faulty blood—"

"He was sympathetic."

"He knows how tempting it is to depersonalize patients. He knows what it's like having death on your hands."

"So you chatted about having death on your hands."

"Fuck off, Duncan."

"Go on."

"So we got talking about growing up Irish Catholic and being a kid in Iran. How dirty toilet paper seems when you've always washed with water. How his cousin used to hide herself when a man came on television, just as she wrapped up in a chador to go out in the street. How he used to roll up in a filthy carpet to sleep in his uncle's taxi in the middle of winter, no better than the slave of this old man with a cossack mustache, and his mother, how she got onto a bus to join his father in Germany, and his brother was born, and they never sent for him. And Mehdi's eyes filled up and I could feel the courage in him, never mind all the pain, and he ended up in my arms. I wanted to make up for all that hurt—in me too. In both of us."

"Go on."

"It was eerie. I didn't have to think, my body just sort of took over. He was so caring."

"Just another killer orphan from Iran."

"Oh bullshit!" she stormed. "How do you know what he's done?"

"That's what we're trying to establish."

"You want to hound him. You'll push him till he goes off and shoots himself."

"Speaking of which. Whatever happened to your father's pistol?"

"What?"

"Your father. He shot himself, remember? Whatever happened to the pistol he used?"

"What brought that up?"

"It's become important. Where's the pistol now?"

"You're changing the subject. You want to—"

"It ended up in the bedroom on Melrose Street, didn't it."

"If you knew that, if you"—all at once her anger turned cold and incredulous—"you're trying to trap me."

"Trap you?"

"Oh don't be coy with me. Jesus, I hate that about you. Trying to play cat and mouse like some clever TV detective. If I knew anything about a pistol you'd be the first to hear."

"How did the pistol find its way to Jerry's bedroom?"

"It can't be the same one."

"It's the twin of the pistol in a snapshot of you and your father. I borrowed the photo from your aunt. Want a look?"

"This is obscene. Me spying on Mehdi, you spying on me." She scooped up her glass and drained it. I got ready to duck.

"I wasn't expecting to find the photo," I explained. "It begs for an explanation."

"The last time I saw the gun, it was in my mother's dresser in Newton. I was home from Dana Hall. I must have been about fourteen."

"What were you doing in the dresser?"

"I was curious. Spying, if you want. Trying to find out about the real world. Prep school was like being buried alive in a hope chest. The pistol was under a pile of my mother's underwear, in a green tin box with her important papers—marriage license, birth certificates, that stuff. I haven't seen it since."

"What were you doing in the green box?"

"I had the nutty idea that I'd find something about my father. Why he died or what it meant or something."

"Did you?"

"Sort of. My mother'd kept a newspaper clipping. That was something to a kid who'd screened out every single thing."

"Where's the green box now?"

"I have the papers here, except for the ones I gave to the lawyer doing her estate. But no gun."

"Did Jerry know the pistol was there?"

"What would Jerry be doing poking around in my mother's undies?"

"How about searching for documents she was using to blackmail him? Maybe they were bargaining about that when he drove her home, and he gave up and went upstairs to tear through her room. Maybe the pistol presented a tempting solution to his problem."

Carol sloshed wine into her glass, giving me a prosecutorial squint. "Then why are we going after Mehdi at all?"

"Mehdi had the same motive for searching that room as Jerry did. And I suspect he was with Jerry about the time he died, so he could've planted the pistol."

"Isn't it possible my mother gave Jerry the pistol for some reason?"

"It's just as possible she gave it to Mehdi to protect his house when he started receiving hate mail."

"God," she choked, "how could Mehdi—I mean, *Mehdi* of all people—?"

The wash began to spin. The tremor spread through the room. When Carol put her glass down on one of the coin boxes, it began shimmying toward the edge. She picked it up with a disgusted sputter:

"You like the suspense, don't you. Just like the conceited jackasses I work with at the hospital. Gushing over some 'really intriguing' syndrome."

I reached for the wine bottle and, while I was at it, my dear and gloriously insecure physician. She stuck a palm in my jaw:

"I don't want your sympathy. Just the wine."

I burst out laughing. She hit the ceiling:

"You—!"

But I couldn't help myself, and the next thing I knew she was smacking me with her fists, splattering wine all over me and her and the cement floor. I fell back against the rumbling washer, snickering idiotically, ducking her fists, making her more furious. Only when she threw a tremendous slap at my left ear did I grab for her wrist, catching and wrenching her little finger. She yelped, then came at me in earnest, elbow and knuckles, wrestling down onto one knee, until I dropped her to the floor and threw myself across her, spilling the rest of my glass. The impact knocked the wind out of her. It also shocked her enough so that she growled, "Get off me, you idiot," smashing one palm into the cement floor in blind frustration.

"Quit it," I said pouncing on the hand. "You'll break a goddamned bone."

"You jackass," she muttered. I let her up. She was digging at her eyes with the heels of her hands. "Pick on someone your own size."

"You damned near broke my eardrum."

"I wish I had."

I snugged her into me, and together we leaned back against the quaking washing machine. A few drops of wine glistened in her hair. She wasn't crying.

"I've got to stop going there, Duncan."

"Come on upstairs."

She put out her arm to check me. "Listen. If I could get you into Mehdi's office, do you think you'd find some definite evidence? One way or the other?"

"It's worth a try."

"Friday night we're going to a concert. I could leave a window in his private office unlocked."

"Perfect."

"Is there an alarm system?"

"I can show you how to shut it off. I helped install it."

"What would you have to find? What would it take to bury your suspicions once and for all?"

"I don't know."

"Oh hell." She got to her feet grumbling: "Why did you have to drag me into this mess?"

I reached up under her hem and caught her thigh: "Never give up."

"You're so romantic," she said pushing an armload of soggy laundery down at me. "I can't stand it."

But she came into my arms there on the cool cement floor. We rolled up against the door, blocking it, just in case, reaching into each other for all the forbidden feelings we'd been choking back, letting everything go at once. In her excitement Carol kicked the fresh laundry off the chair, and for a moment it was an orgy, the two of us panting and squeezing together there among the damp, disheveled skirts as in a harem of ghostly selves. "Not so fast," I urged, "let's enjoy this."

"Somebody will come in."

"To hell with them."

"After all the other risks, what's one more." She was inside my shirt. I loved the smell of her hair. She whispered something I couldn't hear into my left armpit, so I made her repeat it. She hesitated: "If we ever get through this mess, are we . . . I mean, are you free to, you know—"

"What, love you forever? Marry you?"

"Or are you just using me."

"It would turn my life completely upside down. All hell would break loose. For one thing, it would be the end of my work with Vera. But it could happen. I feel that in my bones. It could happen. Why ask? Interested?"

"I'm afraid I'll fall in love with you." Her shoulders shrugged. "Have."

"Mmm. Me too."

She was fiddling with my belt. "It's a rotten mess."

"I know. I love it."

▽

Chapter Thirty-Four

Midweek Vera phoned. "You've been keeping a low profile in the office," she said dryly. "I hardly notice you."

"You have a very British sense of humor."

"Do I." Not a question.

"My murder has taken a new turn." As I was describing the latest twists, Vera cut me short:

"So you're sending your little duckie off to seduce this Iranian bloke. And then you make her tell you all the details. Oh, that's very professional. I understand perfectly. You're a true scientist, love. Be sure she describes all her sensations for you. All the tingling and swelling—women get erect too, you know. Perhaps you could tumble her yourself. You never know what messages she might hide in her bloomers."

"Vera—"

"And of course an Iranian woodpecker is a rare—"

"Listen. Friday night I'm going to search Dr. Farhat's office. It may turn up evidence about the real-estate scam."

"Fine, love. Just send me your half of the office rent for the month. At your convenience, anytime in the next two hours."

"Vera—"

"And try not to get arrested for invasion of privacy, et cetera. How do you plan to get into this Iranian's office anyway?"

"Dr. Schell's going to leave a window open."

"You trust her?"

"So far."

"You're in this a lot deeper than you think, aren't you?"

"That's a tough question."

"Oh Duncan," she groaned, "what am I doing with a partner who considers that a tough question?"

Friday evening I waited in Meg's room at the hospital for a phone call from Carol. "Have you noticed?" she said. "Rachel hasn't been talking about volunteering for Nicaragua lately."

"See? It doesn't pay to worry."

"Instead she's hinting about dropping out of school to marry Sean."

"We've been talking about it. She'll work it out."

"Maybe you let her see too much of him."

"She also talks about what she might study in college."

"Why doesn't she mention that around me?"

"There's something about you two. Rachel likes to pull your tail. Trust her. Be patient. She needs to feel her choices come out of her, not us. Especially not the mother she's always been so close to."

"I suppose. We've seen this coming since she was a kid. Other people with kids used to warn us. Remember?"

We joked about that, how you can see that particular train coming for miles and yet you still have to make yourself jump out of the way when the time comes. I was giving Meg's hand a squeeze when the phone rang.

It was Rachel at her most enthusiastic. "Hey, listen. A woman just called from the Arab-American Anti-Defamation League, about a guy from over in Waltham. He publishes, like, a hate newspaper called *Heritage* something."

"*Heritage Strike Force.*"

"Right. His name's—"

"I bet his name's Don Frazier."

"Right. Exactly. See, the woman wonders if you're still going to—ahh." The air went out of her balloon. "I suppose you've already checked him out."

"But I forgot to tell Mrs. Baroodi that."

"Oh well."

"But I like your attitude."

"You should've called her. Boy, if I was as careless as you, would I ever hear about it."

"Sorry, kid."

After I hung up I said to Meg, "Don't feel picked on. My tail just got pulled too." I pointed to the birthday card on her nightstand: "At least you got a birthday card out of her."

"That's not from Rachel. That's a chiropractic birthday greeting from your pal Mehdi Farhat."

The card showed a vertebral giraffe dancing on the computer-personalized letters HAPPY BIRTHDAY MARGARET. Nobody ever called Meg by the name on her birth certificate. "Mehdi's a hustler," I said, "grant him that."

"Maybe he cares," Meg scolded. "He's going to help me get moving again once I'm ready for physical therapy."

"For free?"

Before she could answer the phone killed the question. I reached for it: "That's for me."

"We're at Symphony Hall," Carol muttered in my ear. She sounded tense, rushed, conspiratorial: "It's Pops. *Orpheus in the Underworld* and a bunch of junk. I'll try to steer us to a restaurant afterward, but I can't guarantee how late we'll be. Work fast."

"I'll try. The alarm off?"

"I turned the knob all the way to the right, like you said, and the little red light went off. And the window facing away from the house is unlocked. It opens inward. Be careful."

"You're terrific."

Her voice turned to dust in her throat. "Got to go. Mehdi's coming."

The receiver clicked.

I kissed Meg's cheek. She tried to catch my eye: "What was that all about?"

"Got work to do."

As I turned to go she blurted out: "Is it true about the gunshots?"

"I don't hear any gunshots."

"Don't play dumb, Duncan. That stirs up my worst fears. I mean, bullets fired at the house. You asked Rachel not to tell me."

"I thought you had enough worries."

"How serious is it?"

"Cosmetic damage, that's all. I'll get the door repaired."

"Never mind the door. How serious is the situation?"

"So far it's just intimidation."

"So far? Where does it end?"

"Either the case will break soon or I'll be quitting."

"I hope you know what you're doing."

"Fear not, dear Margaret."

"Last time you gave me that baloney it was me who ended up visiting you in the intensive-care ward."

"Don't you have any faith in me?"

"I worry about Rachel. All you have to be is a little wrong. Even one percent killed is too much."

In the starry dusk I slipped through Mehdi's shrubbery toward the old carriage house. If anyone challenged me, I could say I'd been working for Mehdi. But the gray lawn was deserted. The boss's Caddy was gone. The junior chiropractors had all punched out for the weekend. A lone lantern on a post turned the doorway yellow. I crouched in the shrubbery locating the basement window.

It was small. As Carol had promised, it swung inward to the touch. Going in feet first on my stomach, I found it a tight squeeze. The sill was sharp. To clear the flashlight, notebook, and minicamera in my sportscoat pocket I had to flatten my chest. I pushed backward and down, legs dangling now, toes feeling for the floor. Just as I emptied my lungs, I felt my legs catch. Caught in something. And suddenly I realized the something was alive, moving. More exactly, it was tangling up my legs, wrapping them. I gave a grunt and a kick, grabbing for the window frame to extricate myself.

Hands were binding my legs. I pulled mightily at the window frame, kicking for a face or groin, only to have gravity and the weight of an unseen body drag me down into the dark. The window frame jabbed in my armpit and scraped my ribs. At this angle I couldn't get a grip. I took a chance.

"Lay off! It's me, Duncan Ames. I work for Dr. Far—"

Cotton jammed into my face, a wad big as a catcher's mitt, cold, bitter-tasting, medicinal—*ether*.

I wrenched my face away, banging my head on the window frame. The hand behind the cotton helped me bang my skull again, and then again. This made the ether more efficient, and I twisted my face from side to side, grabbing at the cotton with both hands, trying to hold my breath, more and more light-headed.

Strong son of a bitch.

Knuckles were drilling into my spine. The pain made me stupid. When I shouted my voice was a feeble boyish quack. I tried to force myself down into the hole once and for all, but the hand kept my head jammed back against the frame, and the pressure in my back seemed to disconnect my legs, so that I was floating in the darkness, paddling with my arms in freezing space. *Let go,* I told myself. *Let go.* But I couldn't stop and my thoughts got lost in the pain. I heard myself gasping, the ether slashing into my lungs. As I was trying to find my body, I fell out of a tree, floating backward into the night sky with a wasp's nest in my arms, crushed into my face, soft and papery, and the soft vicious buzzing in my eyes and up my nose. Then I was flying.

Sinking.

When I hit bottom, my back broke and my breath went away, then in the middle of the pain a shoe was checking my face for signs of life. My hands tried to climb the pantleg. My teeth went for the ankle even as my brain was thinking the futility of it. A kick shook me off, then the cotton pressed down hard, this time going right through my head and out the other side into total blackness.

My lungs wouldn't work. In the blackness I was sucking air through my nose, panting, suffocating. I fought to wake up. My eyes wouldn't work, my jaw was paralyzed. Where were my hands? *Stroke. You've had a stroke.*

Panic jolted me, fear as horrible and meaningless as a hot wire inserted in the brain. Yet I could think. I could still think. I twisted my head back and forth.

Bandage.

My face was wrapped in bandage: eyes, mouth. Hands, too. Probably also feet if I could find them in the jumbled numbness. Elastic sprain bandage, knotted tight. When I shifted I found myself crushed up in a box. It came back to me: he'd trapped me. Blanked me with ether. Dumped me somewhere—a trunk, an empty freezer—until he could get rid of the body. Unless he meant to leave me buried alive because he didn't have the nerve to kill me outright.

More panic, worse than before. I was sorry I'd woken up. How long had it been? Ten minutes? Hours? At least I could move my knees left and right, about a foot each way. I strained this way and that, probing.

A closet maybe. He wouldn't stuff me in a closet to die. Or would he.

Except in unusual circumstances, the investigator should avoid being buried alive. I tried to laugh. Sweat poured off me. Straining to loosen the bandages was only tightening the knots. Though my hands and feet were numb, I tried to feel around.

The sides of the box had the density of sheetrock. The front wall sounded like a hollow-core door: to the touch a hardwood veneer with some kind of glossy varnish. Perhaps he'd stuffed me in a closet in the renovated basement. If so, he'd have to move me before Monday morning.

Take heart, son.

But I was suffocating. My head ached. Pushing upright, I tried to relieve the pressure on my lungs, breathing deeply against the pain. My fingers probed the crack under the door for reassurance. People don't usually asphyxiate in closets. My fingers managed to drag the bandage off my face. This cheered me up a good deal.

With my elbows bound to my sides, my teeth could just reach my wrists. I gnawed at the knots, getting nowhere. For variety I creaked to my feet, an inch at a time, like a climber creeping toward a summit. A shelf stopped my head, but I could breathe. My legs came back. After a while I inched back down, gnawed at the bandage, maybe drifted off for a few minutes, then started up again.

Carol must have fallen apart at the concert. Under pressure she must have spilled everything: had it pried or teased out of her. Or was it worse than that? Was she really jelly, childishly infatuated with the bastard? What was it Dorothy had said to me? *You wouldn't think doctors would be such babies.* Or was it worse even than that?

In my eleventh cycle I found myself daydreaming about a time when the toddling Duncan had locked himself in the trunk of the family Ford and scared his father half to death. It was vivid—I could feel my round-toed leather shoes and the steel ribs of the trunk; the smell of my father's pipe tobacco tickled my nose and I heard his voice just over my shoulder in the blackness of the closet. Wrong memory for this occasion.

I was at the top of my thirty-seventh cycle when footsteps came for me. No light switch snapped. The tangle of fear and relief was sickening. I cocked my hobbled wrists up under my chin for the maximum swing. But when the door opened a flashlight hit me in the eye, and when I swung at the shadowy face behind it I spilled stupidly across the floor at his feet. In a flash the cottony wad of ether was in my face. I tried to play dead but it was too late. His knee crushed my chest and when I gasped for air the ether began smothering me back toward roaring nothingness.

Rats were gnawing at my wrists, tearing tiny chunks out of my hands, yet their saliva kept me from feeling any pain. Hands clamped together as in prayer, I was pounding the little buggers when I woke up. My cheek burned. My face was on the floor of a car, the carpet bristly in my eye. I recognized the musty woodshed smell of the Volvo. My hands and feet were gone again: I was still hog-tied. In the darkness I couldn't make more sense than that.

I came to in a flash of fear, nauseous up to my chin. The car had stopped. The driver's door opened and chunked shut, then the door behind my ear creaked and hands dragged me onto a street. Feet first, I scraped along the asphalt in the dark. Sand and cold pebbles went up the back of my shirt but I let my head wobble, playing dead. No more ether, please. There were two cars idling, the one behind probably the Mercedes.

He moved fast, dumping me at the shoulder of the road. Maybe there was nothing to fear. Teach me a lesson. I could hear water nearby: a stream, maybe a river. I smelled swamp. Overhead a few stars winked. Something—a shoe—crashed into my skull and my thoughts fell apart.

I heard the hiss of a tire valve. Mehdi was flattening a tire on the Volvo. A hubcap clattered on the pavement.

He went into the Mercedes. The door latched. When I cracked my eyelids the headlights were blinding.

"Pull the loose bandage off his neck," Mehdi shouted.

Nobody moved. My neck hurt too much to turn and look for a face.

"Take the bandage," he fumed. "He has to get dirty from the street."

Suddenly the logic of it slammed me. He was staging an accident. He meant the car to break my neck.

I tried to feel my hands and my legs.

The engine revved, the transmission caught with a tiny squeal. My body recoiled. I flung myself onto my shoulder so hard the momentum carried me through the flash of pain and smashed my nose in the dirt. Again I twisted, into grass, and then rolled into taller weeds. I heard the tires squeak. He meant to crush me. I threw myself over again, into a guy wire—phone-pole support—which cut my ribs and hung me up until I could wrench myself into the grass again. The car was moving. I shoved my wrists between my legs, skinnying myself, rolling in weeds and stabbing twigs, down a slope now, faster. The Mercedes backed up and shot toward me again, headlights exploding over my head.

I flung myself downhill, over stones and sticks and stubborn grass, into mud and then freezing water that closed over my head, so heavy and black it seemed to be inside my skull too. After some wallowing I got up on my knees biting at the bandage on my wrists. But he was running in the grass, too close, so I floundered out into the river, throwing myself ahead into the current, under the suffocating water. I rolled onto my back, trying to let the water carry me in a dead man's float, but I couldn't control the motion and my face kept plunging into the freezing water. Not much current: I was wallowing in tar. I was sinking in heavy black tar.

He would drown me.

I forced myself to lie dead in the water, gasping for air. My wet clothes were dragging me down. Panic thrashed through me, and I tried to beat it back, kicking upward with all my body, feeling myself tangle in underwater weeds. My face cleared the surface and I filled my lungs for another plunge, but this time something stopped my feet. Earth. Riverbottom. I hadn't gone anywhere.

He was searching for me along the shore. Footsteps hissed in the grass along the bank. The headlights fanned across the river. I let myself sink until only my mouth remained above the surface. Underwater I fought to pry the bandage off me, but I couldn't get a grip on it.

The cold was shaking me apart. I clamped my jaw shut and forced myself to give in to the spasms: *Think warm. Think hot sun on your back.* Mehdi's voice said, "I see him."

I choked down my breath.

"Help me look."

Lying on my back I pushed along beside the shore, heels in the spongy river bottom. He was running along the bank muttering. My nose was full of water. The moon winked out of the dirty clouds and he began running in the shallows, rechecking the weeds, back and forth like a hunting dog. I sat up in the water, only my face showing. My fingers picked at the bandage around my ankles.

"There!"

He came wading at me. With a furious kick I plowed into the current. I rolled onto my stomach, scooping water under me in a spastic dog paddle, pulling myself through the river. I heard him running in great splashes, catching up, very close. He brushed against my foot.

I plunged toward the bottom, grabbing at weeds to pull myself under, lunging underwater from stalk to stalk, yanking up weedy clumps. When my lungs were splitting, I let myself float. The splashing was a couple yards behind me. My hands kept up a frantic puny sculling, dragging my useless legs. Then he threw himself at me in the chest-high water.

Again I dived, but too shallow, and when I floundered to the surface he got a grip on my belt. I stabbed at him with my feet. He toppled over holding on to my belt with one hand, pulling me under. So I let myself go and the momentum sank him. I looped my arms over his ears and squeezed. After an instant of shock his body flew into a panicky rage: arms, legs, ragged fingers. His wristwatch slashed across my throat. I rode him underwater, knees in his armpits, trying to drown him. Then his head bucked out of my grip and I lost him. When he burst into the air I threw my knotted fists at his face. The impact seemed ridiculous, like pounding a wet mattress, but he lost his balance again. I didn't wait around.

As I thrashed out into the current, I heard him sweeping his arms about him in the water, flustered. He couldn't swim. That was it. He couldn't swim. In the rippling silence he sloshed toward the riverbank.

I humped clumsily through the water, unable to let up without sinking. Farther out the current picked up. It carried me under a railroad trestle, where I reached for one wooden piling, desperate to catch my breath, and banged head first into another. I took a quick tour of the solar system and nearly didn't come back.

For a few minutes I flailed about in the current, my teeth rattling in my skull. The first time I touched bottom I forced myself upright and hobbled toward shore. Slithering up into the grass I collapsed, letting the cold shake me by the throat, too exhausted to care.

I rocked back and forth hugging my knees and shivering. It was cold. Time to get the bandages loose before my extremities dropped off. I thought about the Volvo's heater. With my luck he would be waiting for me, using the car as bait. But I had to cut the knots.

In the end I hopped across the road to a mailbox on a post and sawed my wrists back and forth against the tin flag. A few strands frayed, then the first layer let go. I unwrapped the rest with my teeth. After a while my hands began burning with nerve pain coming back to life, and I was able to free my legs.

I scouted out the Volvo.

Nobody.

No key either. So no heater. And not much sense changing the deflated tire. I wrapped myself in the wool lap blanket from the back seat and started strolling. My teeth rattled. The water in my shoes squeaked.

Between stands of pines were lawns like pastures and houses dead still in the moonlight: places whose expensive owners would have you arrested if you asked to use the phone. A horse whinnied. No traffic. No cops. No neighbors beating a conga drum under a streetlight.

Maybe a half hour later I came to a town common. No public signs: if you don't know where you are, you don't belong here. Drugstore, town hall, police station. War memorial with beaky bronze eagle flapping over a list of dead men. Town of Dover. Refuge of old Yankees and new money, maybe fifteen miles into the Boston suburbs. At a pay phone, I dialed Rachel. To my joy Vera answered. "Rachel's asleep. Where are you?"

I told her. "What time is it?"

"Three-thirty."

"I've lost my car keys."

"For pity's sake, Duncan. You're slurring everything. Are you drunk?"

"I'm freezing wet. Bring me some dry clothes."

"How about hot coffee?"

"I love your voice."

"You are drunk."

"I'm damn glad it's you."

"You're raving, love. Try to keep your wits about you for another twenty minutes."

Chapter Thirty-Five

"He tried to kill me."

"Who?"

"Mehdi Farhat. Let's drive." I climbed into the back of Vera's station wagon and began changing clothes out of my duffel bag. "And somebody else was there."

"Your friend Carol?"

"I couldn't see."

"What do you think?"

"I don't know what would be worse. If she was there, I'll wring her neck. If not, Mehdi may have already wrung it."

"Oh." Meaning: *I warned you.*

"I've just spent an inspirational evening entertaining second thoughts about this case."

"You want to tell me about it over some hot food?"

"No, I want to make up for lost time. Head for Boston while I change."

"Can you go to the cops?"

"Not without evidence."

"What's wrong with your car?"

"Nothing. Mehdi's got my keys. He was going to break

my neck and make it look as if I got picked off changing a flat."

"It wouldn't have worked."

"All depends how sharp the local cops are." I climbed over the front seat. "Good thing you decided to visit."

"I told you I wanted to see for myself what you were up to. If you just listened to me once in a while."

"Step on it. We shouldn't get a ticket at this hour."

At the least Carol had collapsed. Conceivably Mehdi had even turned her around. There were other possibilities, too, each uglier than the one before.

In the hour before dawn Brigham and Women's Hospital was sleepwalking. Under dimmed lights nurses were going about preop chores while patients snatched scraps of sleep. At the nurses' station on Meg's floor I found an intern I recognized from the day shift. The curly-headed Dr. Gary Ellmann was shmoozing with one of the nurses, a doe-eyed blonde with a discouraging Slavic name and a heroic brassiere. "You're early for visiting hours," he tooted. "See the Celtics game last night?"

"I got tied up."

"They got killed."

"The kid down the hall," I said, "Carol Schell's patient, the one with the gunshot wounds. Have they moved him?"

"Tony? He's been discharged."

"Got his address?"

Gary cracked a grin: "You trying to bust him?"

"I need an expert to ask about some bad coke that figures in a case I'm stuck with."

"Not involving Carol's husband by any chance?"

"She's asked me to look into his death."

Gary and the nurse exchanged wise glances. He said, "Carol could have asked Tony for you. They were buddies.

The day he left the kid gave half the floor little packets of coke."

"Good stuff?"

"It passes all the tests."

"Where's he live?"

"You'll have to ask downstairs."

"Give them a call for me. You'll get better treatment than I will."

While Gary phoned I introduced myself to the nurse, Irene Unpronounceable. "When interns are on all night," I asked, "do they get to nap at all?"

"If it's quiet."

"Is it a private spot?"

She blushed: "You mean, like, do people fool around there?"

"Suppose you got up and went out for a walk. Would anyone notice you were gone?"

"If we needed you for an emergency, like if somebody coded, we'd really be after you."

"Let's have a look."

Two cots squeezed behind curtains at one end of a staff room. There were a few lockers and a Coke machine. "If you were sleepwalking," I said, "you might step out and not be missed."

"Everybody's usually too pooped to go anywheres. But it's possible."

"Who'd know if Dr. Schell took a nap last Friday night?"

She shrugged: "It'd be simplest to, like, just ask Carol. You know?"

From a laundry cart I picked up a uniform, baggy white trousers, and jacket. "Let me borrow these till this afternoon."

"That's hospital property." She was flustered. "I mean, they have to be washed."

"I only need them for ten minutes. For my investigation."

"Are you doing internal review? Malpractice?"

"I'm not allowed to discuss these things. Sorry."

I thanked Irene, took the uniform and Tony D'Agostino's address, and clipped out the door into the murky dawn.

Vera headed across Mission Hill into Dorchester. On the hill the sky was a critical gray, neither night nor morning, and I felt like a rat in a shoe box, ready to spring when the lid came off.

The house was the healthiest-looking one on its block: a side-by-side with asphalt siding in a ruddy brick pattern. A bald snow tire sat in the supermarket cart on the front porch, but otherwise the place was tidy as a TV commercial. Trees had overgrown the vacant lot next door, something that in Boston could happen only in a poor neighborhood. As I got into my uniform Vera clucked. "What's with the hospital getup?"

"I've got surgery to perform. Sit tight."

After the doorbell played reveille for the fifth time, a woman came to the door in a deep-maroon robe. Behind butterfly-framed bifocals, her eyes winced at the daylight. Two chains secured the door, top and bottom. The woman eyed the hospital whites with shrewd amazement, absently tugging one strand of gray hair as she talked.

"What's the big idea? Something happen to Tony?"

"Where is he?"

"Tony's not here."

"This is an emergency. A woman's life is in danger."

"What woman?" Suspicion sharpened Mrs. D'Agostino's eye as if she were seeing the snake in Eden.

I said, "Dr. Schell at Brigham and Women's Hospital. She tried some cocaine Tony gave her and collapsed. She's in gross systemic shock. We need to find out exactly what she ingested."

"Tony don't deal drugs anymore. That's all done with." Mrs. D'Agostino squinted. I was an apparition to her, real and unreal at the same time, like the idea of death.

I pushed: "Listen to me. If Carol Schell dies, your son will never see daylight again, I guarantee you."

"She's a doctor. She had no business taking no substances."

"It was Tony's gift. She couldn't know what was in it."

"If I tell you where he's at, you won't sic cops on him."

"Stop fooling around."

"He's at Melonee's apartment. She has this little baby now, and Tony's being a good—"

"What's the address. Quick."

She told me the street. She was still advertising Tony's manly virtues as I ducked back into the car.

Melonee's little baby was partying on the top floor of a triple-decker tenement with half a dozen reclining guests. My nose told me somebody was storing a basket of dead eels in the hall closet. Madonna was whining about love in stereo.

Melonee met me in the doorway with her little baby growing out of her left hip and singing along with Madonna. I pressed past them. "Hey," Melonee objected, "nobody called the Emergency."

The guests seemed to have dropped in their tracks on the carpet, in two beanbag chairs, on the duct-taped vinyl sofa. They looked at me with parted eyes, dreaming they were awake, watching far-off mountains turn into clouds.

They gawked at me, full of vacant bliss, too old for lullabies, too young for last rites. No sign of Tony. Melonee's little baby wagged its arms and sang its lungs out. Its mother followed me across the room, young and skinny in a pair of peach-colored underpants with a lipstick kiss sewn on one hip. Adolescent apology squirmed in her voice.

"The baby's kept us up all night."

Tony wasn't in the kitchen either. Melonee recovered enough to fuss at me:

"You can't just walk in here, you know." And when he proved not to be in the bedroom either, she added, "You can just get out of here, mister. Get out!" Nor on the plastic-sheeted rear porch. "Get out!" she cried, tugging at my white sleeve. "Out!"

Which is when Tony bellowed from the bathroom, "Hey, what the fuck!"

Hello.

He was on his back in a full tub of steamy water studying a glossy fan magazine about porn movie stars. More magazines and a big glass of tomato juice sat on a TV tray set across the tub rim. He had the diamond in his ear and lazy eyes.

I took him up out of the water like a poached carp, spilling his juice and drowning his books. His lips went round in a carp's stupefied pout. While I had the initiative, I straightened his back out against the wall. "What're you doing?" he complained. "I just got stitches out."

Two thin purplish ridges slanted above his belly button where the stitches had been.

"That coke you gave Carol Schell," I said releasing him, "what was in it? Her husband's had a heart attack."

"Hey, that's not my fault."

"Tell me what was in it. Maybe we can revive him."

"How'd you know I— Did Carol tell you?"

"What was it—coke spiked with what?"

"Nothing, man. Just primo stuff. I wouldn't give Carol bad shit. I told her, you don't need to cannonball with this stuff, it's like a lifetime supply. The best. You look at a few grains, you're gone."

"Her husband's heart has stopped."

"Somebody said. Is he on a machine?"

"We have to move fast."

"I *like* her, man, she saved my ass in that hospital. I had bullet holes here and here and—" When he noticed my face he flinched. "When she asked, I gave her primo. What she wanted."

"She asked you."

"Shit yes. Couple weeks ago. Big, big rush. In the middle of the night she came over here to get it from Melonee. She showed Melonee this trick with diaper cream—you know, the white goo? —well it gets rid of warts. See, for years Melonee had this humungus wart on her—"

"Carol gave you cash?"

"I didn't want to charge her. Just what it cost me."

"You're a philanthropist, Tony."

"Doctors got money up the ass. And I got this baby to—"

He sank onto the pink mother-of-pearl toilet seat, water still dripping from his nose and hands and shriveled penis. His chin sank into his hand as if trying to remember something, some chore, some crucial bit of wisdom whispered in his ear as he walked out the door in another life, on another planet, a long time ago.

No lights in Carol's windows. Against the overcast sky Yuppie Towers looked empty as the Bunker Hill monument. Nobody answered Carol's phone. Sunday-morning stillness hovered over the Farhat hacienda too. No Mercedes in the garage. At one point Sari came out and planted croquet wickets in the lawn, but then she shrank back into the house. "It's way too quiet," I said. "Something's up."

"You should ring up Rachel," Vera reminded me. "And we haven't had any breakfast."

Mr. Donut greased us and offered a pay phone. Then we headed back to the hospital to return my borrowed uniform and loiter. As any moron could have foretold, a pinch-hitter showed up for Dr. Schell's shift: Dr. Lopez, a Spanish-inflected gent low in the hospital pecking order and eager to please. A week ago Dr. Schell had arranged some days off—for an interview with a foundation that sends young doctors to Africa. "Africare," said Dr. Lopez with a snap of the fingers, "that's the name." "A free care," he pronounced it. "In Toronto, I think."

It was Sunday in Toronto too, and humanitarian foundations there weren't taking emergency calls.

"Why so upset?" Vera asked. "If she's not really going to Toronto, so what?"

"Maybe she's off on a love trip with a wineskin and Omar the Chiro."

"So? Do I sense bruised male vanity?"

"It hurts to think they might have been planning all along to kill me."

"How long is all along?"

"At least one week." *How long?* I felt the question fluttering about my ears and I couldn't catch it. *How long?* "Come on, let's go meet the relatives."

"What relatives? Where?"

"Auntie and Unk. Hyde Park. Let's go."

Mr. Clancy's Chevrolet was already dripping clean in his driveway, but otherwise nothing had changed on McDermott Avenue since last Sunday. The *Herald American* sports page filled the vinyl lounger, Mr. Clancy's red-faced scowl above it, wide-cuff chino pants sticking out below. Only silky blue socks with tiny silver seals on them told you Mr. C had been to Mass earlier. The eyes watched Gladys tuck us into the tidy living room.

When I came to my question, Gladys took a deep breath, put on her endearing granny smile, and sat down on the organ bench. "Well," she said, "Carol and Dr. Farhat are bound to be close. After all, she sort of grew up in that house of his."

"That's no answer," I said.

"Well it certainly is true," Gladys piped.

"Trash," Mr. C growled. He didn't look up.

"Beg your pardon?" Vera responded.

"He means," said Gladys, "that Carol and Dr. Farhat have always been chummy."

"What I mean is, her mother used her." Mr. C's voice was low and fierce, like a drill boring through rock miles under the earth. Gladys hurried to explain.

"Carol used to baby-sit for the doctor and his wife. Before the divorce."

"Only that?" I asked.

"Why fiddle around," Mr. Clancy demanded. "That Arab's had Carol as his pussycat since she was a teenager. And your family knew it, too. Every damn one of them." A sudden rise in his moral blood pressure made Mr. C's face hotly beefy. "How do you think Dorothy got all them perks? It was all arranged, oh so cozy, believe you me. Don't look so surprised."

Gladys flinched: "Now don't go giving the wrong impression."

"What impression?" her husband shot back. "There she was, just a girl, staying there night after night, bold as the Queen of Sheba."

"As far back as college?" I asked.

"Maybe before, for all I know. In her last year at that big-shot prep school she all of a sudden couldn't get good grades. Her, who'd always been a whiz kid."

Gladys took a big breath: "But—"

"That's what that Arab's divorce was all about, if the truth is known. They went to Europe together, the two of them, bold as brass. Visited his brother in Germany. Brought back all these cases of wine. Plus some Oriental rugs. Plus that fancy car, the BMW. Just like a lawful husband and wife."

"But—"

His voice overrode his wife with mixed admiration and disgust: "Gladys would do anything to protect her family."

She didn't argue.

By late afternoon the sun was sneaking looks under the blanket of overcast. In Brookline, the sudden light pointed out a storefront stuccoed to suggest Greek columns and gingerbread doodles on the fine old houses. Two fat red cardinals were grazing on Dr. Farhat's lawn. Sari was galloping back and forth, hammering croquet balls across the sleek grass as if it were polo.

"Hey, Duncan, you want to play this game?"

"Sure. Your father home?"

"Uh-uh. He's gone. Here, you use the blue."

Sari had set up all the wickets in a single long row: strait is the gate. I introduced Vera, and for a few minutes the three of us attacked the wooden balls. Sari knocked into me and let out a whoop. "Good shot," I said. "What time will your father be back?"

"He's gone to my uncle's."

"In Germany?"

"Uncle Ari has all the rugs in the world in his house, all rolled up with strings on them. He knows how to tie this knot, see, so when he wants to show a rug, he just pulls it once, and *zip,* it rolls open. He's got this one rug with trees on it big as the woods where Hansel and Gretel find the witch." Sari sounded rigidly cheerful. "Dina's going to sleep downstairs till my mother gets here."

Dina was the housekeeper. Mehdi wasn't just stepping out overnight. "Did Carol go with him?"

"See, my mother's coming here from California." From the flower-patch pocket on her skirt Sari drew a snapshot of a woman in a satiny pantsuit the same metallic blue color as her eyeshadow, lipstick red as a cardinal's backside. The woman wore her black hair in blond-tipped ringlets. Her style was supposed to be elegantly carefree, but she held herself as if she were lugging a twenty-pound tiara on her noggin.

"Did Carol go with your father?" I asked.

Sari placed the croquet balls together, stepped on hers, and with a two-fisted chop sent mine skipping across the lawn toward Katmandu. With the same rigid cheer she shrugged: "I don't know. They had a fight."

"When did he go?" Vera asked.

Sari took aim at Vera's bright-orange ball and swung, but this time her ball bolted off wildly into the shrubbery. "Didn't you see him?" she demanded. "You just drove right by him."

"Going to the airport?"

"Sure. You can't walk over the ocean, dummy."

"What airline?"

"The one that goes to Germany with the German name."

"Lufthansa."

"Sure."

Vera and I exchanged glances. I handed over my mallet.

"Oh come on," Sari protested. "Let's play croquet." "Croak-it," she called it. "I didn't mean to say you were dumb. I'm sorry, okay? Hey, come *on*."

She stamped her foot. Sooner or later, you could see, there would be tears. "We'll play later," I said. "First I have to talk to your dad."

"I'm sorry I said you were stupid."

"It's okay," I soothed.

"You're not stupid," she persisted. "You're real smart."

"I'm not mad at you."

"I'm sorry," she begged. "Sorry sorry sorry sorry sorry." As I turned for one last wave she was standing in the thickening dusk, waving the croquet mallet like a war club, still screaming: "I'm sorry!"

Chapter Thirty-Six

"Do we have to run?" Vera panted.

"Get in."

I winged across Brookline leapfrogging the last Sunday drivers. Lights were coming on across the city.

"Look for a dark-red Mercedes with his name on the vanity plate."

If they reached Logan, airport security would make it hard to slow them down. If they got out of the country, forget it.

As we were coming out of the Callahan Tunnel darkness was choking up the sky and in my haste I nearly ran over the Mercedes. He was alone. Perhaps he planned to meet Carol in the departures lounge. He took the cutoff before the airport, leading us through East Boston streets to a commercial long-term parking lot. At the automatic gate, he took a ticket and headed toward the back fence.

"Can you get his passport away from him?" I asked Vera.

"You don't want much, do you? Let me see what I can do."

"Be careful."

Vera got out. I parked down the line from Mehdi. The

airport minibus was just making a stop and Mehdi was rushing to catch it. With a briefcase under one arm he stooped slightly to lock the Mercedes. From the trunk he hauled two fat suitcases with little wheels attached. As I moved toward him, keeping low, I heard Vera's polite official tones:

"Good evening, sir. Lot security. Will it be a domestic or international flight this evening?" Vera flashed some sort of ID at him. I couldn't hear his reply. She went on, "Just a preliminary screening. May I see your passport?" Whatever Mehdi said, she answered, "Of course. But better a bit of bother than a hijacking, hmm?"

From his breast pocket he produced a passport. When he turned to close the Mercedes' trunk Vera started walking.

"Let me just check you off." She came over and handed me the passport. I pocketed it.

"Why don't you wait in the car," I said to her. "And lock it. Sometimes tourists get testy when a flight's canceled."

Mehdi wasn't expecting me. In fact he was so startled he offered me a bite of his briefcase, which I declined though the thing nearly broke my left arm. I'd imagined administering a dignified poke in the nose if it came to that, but thanks to the briefcase I exploded. If I'd been a dog I would have ripped his head off. Luckily he sat right down on the gravel clutching his ribs and I caught myself up short, as amazed as he was. He didn't curse me and I didn't apologize.

"Come on, get up." I supervised him with my foot. "Where's Carol?"

He balked: "Give me my documents."

"Where's Carol?"

"My plane is leaving."

I stepped back: "Don't let me keep you."

"Give me the passport."

"We can talk in the car."

He raised his voice: "I want the police."

People at the minibus stop were taking an interest in us. Down the row there was a break in the security fence and I went for it. He came after me in a running crouch, shoes pattering in the gravel, and I turned just in time to catch him reaching for my throat. He was a better fighter with a bottle of ether in one hand. I piled into him, heaving him back against the fence. He managed a hatchet chop at my neck. I staggered backward through the gap in the fence, Mehdi on my heels.

We went alongside a garage dodging junk—cable spools, broken shovel, toilet bowl, transformer boxes bursting with wires as if a space shuttle had blown up over East Boston. Around the corner I found a white-haired gent in suspenders sitting on his back doorstep in a folding chair, smoking a cheroot. When I waved he nodded courteously: *"Buona sera."*

I opened his front gate and ducked across the street between a couple warehouses and came out on a wharf. Between the punky timbers under my feet the black filth of the harbor was sucking at the shore. I smelled creosote and swamp. Up ahead a pile of used tires taller than I was blocked the wharf. End of the line. A jet grunted out of the heavens, unbelievably loud, landing lights blazing. For a moment it hung motionless over my head and I had the giddy feeling I was frozen in a travel poster with unattainable wings bound for an impossible destination.

I spun about waving the passport. Mehdi spat at me.

"Do that again," I said, "and you'll swim to Germany."

"What do you want?"

"Where's Carol?"

He shrugged.

"Why did she kill Jerry Schell?"

Mehdi began brushing at his natty suit. He was winded. "It was—an accident. Jerry was too . . . hungry."

"Carol brought him a lethal dose of cocaine."

"Jerry was full of negative forces. In layman's words—"

"She killed Jerry to protect you."

Mehdi swatted disgustedly at the invisible dirt on his pants. "Protect me from what?"

"You and Jerry were raiding the Carter estate. And he was threatening to tell the world."

"What is this raiding? A procedure. A questionable judgment. No big crime. Maybe somebody pays a fine. You don't kill someone over it."

"You might if he knew you'd murdered Dorothy O'Hare."

"Why should I do such a thing to Mrs. O'Hare?"

"Perhaps because she was squeezing you. Perhaps she knew how that nursing-home fire started."

In the gloomy dusk I felt him smirk.

"That's when you first invented the American Satan, wasn't it? After you'd torched the nursing home?"

"Duncan, I'm receiving very negative emanations from you."

"Wait till you feel the DA's."

"The fire was not me." Mehdi hunkered down. He stared across the filthy silver water at the city lights, still getting his breath. Mosquitoes were breeding in the tires and the air was alive with hungry whines. "After the fire," he said, "there really did come a phone call from some American Satan. And that gave us the idea."

"Including shooting at my house."

"I never did such a thing."

"And your house?"

"That was for sure the stupidest thing. I thought it would stop your suspicions. I never expected to shoot the water pipe in my wall. We only wanted to keep you going in circles."

"Why bother if you have nothing to hide?"

"I am not a criminal."

"You're what I'd call an eighteen percent crook."

He snorted: "Even right now, you look in the face of it and you don't see it."

"You were there when Jerry died. That makes you an accessory."

"This is just guessing."

"When you got home that night you set Sari's alarm clock back an hour, then you woke her up. So she'd think you'd never left the house. But then you forgot to reset the time."

"Ah." He brushed at the mosquitoes swarming in his face. "You're wrong, Duncan. For sure. I tell you something. Jerry was full of negative energies about his interpersonal being. Very depressed. But what happened to him was an accident."

"Like a Mercedes driving over your face."

He winced. "That was stupid."

"Because I'm still alive?"

"It was to scare you. To stop your questions."

"Yeah, well. Death reduces your curiosity all right."

"Carol thinks I would have killed you."

"She's right."

"I'm angry you would think that."

"Where is Carol?"

"Give me the passport."

"Is she going to Germany with you?"

He swatted at the biting twilight around his face. I was starting to itch myself. He said, "I don't need Carol."

I saw my opening: "She's the heart of this, isn't she?"

"These bugs are devils." He was slapping himself with frantic hands.

"Your plane won't wait forever. Tell me the truth."

"The patient is sick," he said grimly. "Carol knows that."

"Knows what?"

"Things are not going to get better. And this time I can't save her. She knows that too."

"What patient?"

"She's sick of it. You know? Really sick."

"Sick of what?"

"The whole thing. The deaths. The mother. It all begins and ends with the mother. Everything."

He hunkered there on the rotting wharf as if talking to himself. In the weakening light I saw the silhouette of the little kid left behind in Tehran years before when his mother had vanished in a gritty billow of smoke from an old city bus. Somewhere across the harbor in the high-rise skyline were Carol's unlit windows, and behind them a calendar sunset, coldly red. I felt a faraway roar of alarm coming toward me. "Look," I said, "Carol's in real trouble, isn't she?"

He nodded. He was picking mosquitoes off his cheek and hands like bits of dirt. "I think when I come back from Europe maybe she has ended it."

"Where is she? She's not at her place and not at the hospital."

"Give me the passport."

He stuffed it into his breast pocket. I asked, "Well?"

It seemed to me he shrugged: "I would guess the mother's house."

Chapter Thirty-Seven

Out in Newton the darkness wasn't fooling around. I was already out of the car before I could tell her BMW wasn't parked in the driveway. To Vera I said, "If Carol's here, I should try talking to her alone."

But the front door was locked. Each time I turned the old-fashioned thumbscrew the bell clattered noisily, but no one answered. When I went back to the car Vera said, "I could swear there's light behind the shade up there. Just faint. Do you see?"

This time I went out back and up the steep slope toward the school, hoping to get a better look at the upstairs windows. I made two discoveries up there. In Dorothy O'Hare's bedroom window a weak gray light flickered. And behind me in the corner of the schoolyard reserved for staff parking sat Carol's BMW. Park up there after hours and you could slip into the house by the backdoor, unseen from the street. The last doubts died.

I broke the window in the back door.

The darkness inside smelled musty. In these few weeks of disuse the house had started to grow strange. Shouting her name I groped through the dark rooms to the stairs. It was possible she would have a weapon. I took the stairs two at a time, hoping sheer momentum would carry me through.

But she was in Dorothy's room, laid out on the high double bed like a patient on the operating table. Under a bedsheet printed with clouds one hand lay tucked between her legs as if she had been trying to excite herself when she passed out. On a portable TV in the corner a little Puerto Rican kid, no more than a first-grader, was lip-synching a Top 40 hit, humping the mike. Behind her glittered a mess of silver stars.

They weren't the stars Carol was seeing. Under the pleated pink lampshade on the nightstand were five pill containers more empty than full. No label on any of them. On the floor were wadded tissues, a half-spilled box of scented baby powder, and a bunch of candy wrappers: gold-foil Easter bunnies and a few Hershey kisses. Under her she had Dorothy's electric blanket at its hottest setting.

She groaned when I shook her, glassy-eyed. "Come on, kid," I grunted, hoisting her up. Printed on her bare back was the pattern of the electric blanket's wires. "You need a stomach pump. Let's see who's on duty tonight in Emergency."

She shook her head: "No, no, all bewful."

"You can't stand up."

When I let go she fell on herself, all twisted, like a puppet. The second time I pulled her up she gave me a lovely imbecile smile and collapsed again:

"Too much gravity in this room. Patient suffers from stage-two gravity disease. Write that down."

"What kind of pills did you take?"

"Good kind."

I dragged her off the mattress: "Upsy-daisy, bewful."

"Can't dance. Love to but I have blister."

"Come on," I grumbled. "You're falling all over me."

"Truth is I don't really know how. Studying to be a doctor."

"Stand up," I barked. "Straighten up."

"Who farted?"

"Pay attention. Walk."

"You loved Jesus you wouldn't fart. If you loved Jesus you wouldn't have to digest plants and animals inside you."

"I'll keep that in mind."

"Oh no. You'd go crazy. Turn into a doctor. Or a nun. See, you chew up animals. And dissolve them in stomach acid. And then fart them and shit them out, all so you won't die. So you can have one more day alive. And when you run out of life you beg doctor for more. It's the truth."

"Too many chocolate Easter bunnies for you."

"Poor beans."

"What?"

"Human beans. Easter beanies." She was giggling like a schoolgirl.

In the bathroom the sudden lights offended her. I forced her head down into the sink and helped her right hand, sticky with Easter bunny chocolate, down her throat. She gave a few painful, ragged heaves, then she began jerking her hand free, fighting me: "Cuh-ow."

"Heave those pills up."

"Get off me, you shit."

"You trying to kill yourself?"

She called me names, trying to throw me off. She flung her whole body backward, and I caught her just as her skull was about to crack against the toilet bowl. I hugged her furiously; I couldn't help it. For some reason this enraged her, and she flailed about so wildly I let go. Lying on the floor, swinging at shadows, she cut her knuckles on the plumbing under the sink, so I straddled her, covering her fists. Since she bucked like an alligator I let my dead weight pin her down. Then her eyes suddenly startled open and she tried to bite my nose.

"It's okay," I murmured. "I know about your mother."

"Fuck off, Duncan."

"The only thing I don't know is why."

"You couldn't. Never could."

She was kicking. Her heel crunched the wicker wastebasket. She punted the toilet-paper roll into the bathtub. I bore down, flattening her to the floor again. After a while it quit being a fight to the death and she was limp as wet newspaper.

"Get off my spleen, you jerk," she grunted. I rolled over onto my elbow.

"That first day, it was a mistake to tell you that your mother wanted to hire an investigator."

She poked my unshaven chin with her knuckles: "Hair doesn't keep growing after you die. That's a fantasy. Your skin contracts some and the hairs stand out. That's all."

I captured her hand in mine. "Right after we talked that day you drove out here from the hospital and parked up by the school. When you got in the house you found Jerry here with your mother. And as soon as he left you brought down the pistol from your mother's dresser. No wonder Jerry panicked afterward. He was accused of something he knew you did."

Her face creased in a dry agony of grief. I said:

"It could explain why you tried to pacify him with the cocaine. And if you killed him, it could explain that too."

She whipped her head back and forth on the pebbly brown linoleum in a spasm of denial. I said:

"I've been talking to Tony D'Agostino."

"Jerry's death was an accident."

"But you left the pistol there. That suggests planning."

"God, I hate you."

"You set up Jerry with the pistol."

"That's not true. After you came snooping around my place the first night, I got scared. I begged Jerry to keep the pistol for me, and he did."

"But Mehdi used the pistol to shoot at his back door. Weeks later."

She grinned: "Borrowed it. One night. We all laughed, you were so . . . So mystified."

"But you planted the pistol on Jerry that last night."

"Poor Jerry. I never expected." Tension tore at her face: "He died. He gobbled it all up. I hate that. The gobbly gobbly. I hated you too. You scared me so much, seeing and seeing and seeing."

"Hating me I understand. But why Dorothy?"

She was shivering: "I don't hate her."

I gave a noncommital shrug: "Yeah, well."

"Oh everybody hated my mother in some way. Me included. But that wasn't much. I mean, she was more me than me. You know? It's in the genes, we're a lot alike. I didn't do it out of hate."

I helped her up and steered us back into the bedroom. In the hall Carol seemed to lean into me, but actually she was pushing us toward her bedroom. It was chilly and dark. I wrapped the quilt around her shoulders and settled beside her on the bed. She shivered, teeth chattering as if she'd fallen through the ice while skating. For a long time we sat there. In the other room TV commercials razzed and passed. Her cheek came to rest on my shoulder.

Finally she said, "My mother had cancer. The day you

met her she was at the hospital for radiation therapy. She was dying and she couldn't bear it, and she lashed out at the rest of us who weren't sick. She blamed Jerry for not making up some money she'd lost in the stock market. She acted as if I'd been sucking the life out of her since I was a baby." She groaned. "See, her thought processes were disordered. Maybe it was tumors; she was scheduled for a brain scan. And then Mehdi. He'd set her up with that investment house. To retire on. But she wanted more. More and more."

"Or she'd reveal the arson?"

"Mehdi had nothing to do with that. He says. But my mother knew all his tricks in the office, the little insurance things."

"I got a taste of that from one of his unhappy patients."

"Mehdi's not a monster. Just hungry. You'd be too, if you'd grown up sleeping on sacks on a garage floor, kicked around like a dog. You'd—"

"And you were his lover all along."

"He was good to me, Duncan. He made me feel I could do anything in the world."

"Like your old man."

"I thought about giving her an injection. But she read my mind, I swear. She wouldn't let me near her with the syringe. It was horrible. And funny. Or maybe I was imagining it. I was certain I'd be found out. If you're a doctor you feel the world is watching your every move." Carol was shaking, sagging against me on the bed. "So in the end it was an impulsive thing."

"But you parked up by the school that day, out of sight. You were planning something."

"I could hear her downstairs digging at Jerry, digging at me."

"That's when you remembered the pistol?"

"Guns make it so easy, you know? It was like a surgical tool or something. A solution."

"But it wasn't just mercy killing, was it."

"No, not just. I thought I understood."

"If I hadn't broken in here tonight, would you have finished off the pills?"

I took her silence as agreement.

"Then it's a good thing you didn't kill me last night."

"It wasn't supposed to happen like that."

"Just put a fright in me."

"I was so scared. So angry at you. But I couldn't, I'd never—"

"But Mehdi could."

"He's jealous of you."

"It was his idea to kill me?"

"He was going to drive the car right up to your neck and then stop. Like the mock executions in Iran. So you'd be so terrified you'd leave us alone. But you messed everything up."

"And then you two had a fight."

"I could've—"

"Killed him."

"It wasn't that bad. He'll be here any minute. We're going to Europe for a while. Get away from this stress."

"He's gone, Carol. Alone."

"See, stress releases poisons that—"

"Listen to me. Mehdi's gone. You're going to have to face this alone."

"He'll be back."

"He'd better have a good lawyer meet his plane."

"I thought he really would run you over. I was sick. I wasn't even afraid anymore. God, I'm shivering." Her voice seemed crushed in her. "For weeks now I've had this funny sensation that I'm dead and spying on everybody."

"Time to pull you back to life, kid." I cradled her, burying her face in my chest, trying to fight her shivers.

"My stomach's so sick."

"You're really sweating."

She staggered into the bathroom again, banging her hip on the doorknob. As I went into Dorothy's room to collect her clothes, I glimpsed Carol hunched over the sink mumbling to herself. Her spine stood out raggedly in the blue fluorescent light. The violence of the spasms made me wince, but she kept at it, elbows squeezing in at her sides and the muscles of her bottom clenching as she labored to expel her demons.

Afterward she leaned on her palms, trembling from head to foot. Under my hands her skin was moist and feverish. I helped her wash up a bit, then I wrapped her in the blanket from her bed. She was glad to be hugged, glad for the warmth, reluctant to get back into her clothes. We settled on the edge of the bed, folded in each other's arms, her forehead on my shoulder. After a while, Carol whispered, "You're not going to let me go, are you."

At the bottom of my throat I grunted the no I couldn't speak.

"Better drag me away then."

"Mmm." Neither of us moved. I had a stupefied sense of the strangeness of our lives. I couldn't think, couldn't move, couldn't change things. Finally, Carol lifted her head.

"Hey," she said softly. "You all right?"

Downstairs I heard Vera's voice calling. I gave Carol one last squeeze. "Come on, Doc. Time to operate."

Chapter Thirty-Eight

"I never thought any place could be so beautiful," Meg said as Rachel and I helped her up the front steps of the house. Vera came up the walk behind us with Meg's travel bag and the radio she'd used in the hospital. Meg looked around in amazement, from the new front door to the sun-chalked red shakes and slightly weather-beaten white window boxes. The familiar sight put a lump in her throat. "It's a miracle."

The sun hung in the neighbors' spruce tree like a runaway kite, and the place breathed in the afternoon hush, trivial and glorious. Meg was radiant:

"Say, who put in the flowers?"

"Rachel planted the window boxes. Like them?"

"They're gorgeous. My favorite colors."

"Green hair, green thumb—they go together."

"You've all been so good to me." Meg gulped. "I wish I'd been able to thank Carol Schell too. She helped me through a lot. Will she ever, you know, be all right?"

"Depends on her trial," I said. "Depends on whether she can ever face up to herself. I think she'll make it. In time." Meg tilted her head to catch my eye. Carol's arrest had shaken Meg in a way I wouldn't have expected. "What about her friend?"

"Mehdi? Odds are, he's drinking a cappuccino about now at a sidewalk café in Freiburg."

"I mean, what happens to him?"

"At the least the heirs to the Carter estate will sue him."

"Is he going to get away with shooting at our house?"

"He swears he didn't do it. And that seems to be the truth." I unlocked the door. "Let's carry you inside."

"Let me try it alone." Meg pushed Rachel's supporting hand away, then suddenly took hold again and kissed it. "Don't misunderstand me, honey."

"It's okay. If I were you, I'd do it too." In the green afternoon light, despite her youth and her vivid convictions—*"You Can't Hug a Child with Nuclear Arms,"* said her T-shirt—Rachel seemed at home in the world these days, or at least not fighting it quite so hard.

Vera reached between us with the house key and pushed the new door open. "Left your keys in the car, Duncan."

For a moment mother and daughter watched me curiously, waiting for me to move. And in the same split second I wondered how I could ever go back to New York. But then Meg suddenly gave a push, and there she was teetering on the threshhold, hand on the door frame. When I went to steady her she waved my hand away: "I have to see if I can do it." She started through the hall into the living room: "Oh it's beautiful in here."

She was really wobbling when Rachel and I, tenderly, without a word, walked her across to the couch. Right away she focused on Rachel's easel by the window:

"You're painting again."

Rachel gave a tongue-tied shrug: "A little drawing."

"That's great."

"You're home," Rachel said. "That's greater."

"I can't wait to get back to work." She had an arm around Rachel's shoulder still. "And I love being home. I love us."

As a threesome we moved to the sofa, more or less rubbing noses. Rachel's eyes were shining: "Anybody else around here starved?"

Vera said, "Security Analysts will cater this reunion. You two sit tight. We'll be right back."

"You three call in the order," I offered, "and I'll go pick it up."

The local Chinese restaurants specialize in sweet-and-sour fat, so I drove over to the Golden Dragon in Framingham, where the spicy cooking lives up to the longevity promised in the fortune cookies. The Dragon provided a viewing window into the kitchen, perhaps designed to counter old wives' tales that there are no stray cats in the neighborhood of a Chinese restaurant. While I waited I watched the cooks slice and dice and rock their woks. Spying on the chefs gave me the funny sensation I was myself being spied on.

Heading home in the dusk, woozy from the fumes of savory chicken, I wasn't paying much attention to the traffic.

A couple blocks from the Dragon where the road is split by a grassy strip and the odd evergreen, I heard a car backfire and felt something hit the back door of the Volvo. A stone.

A bullet.

Across the strip, behind me now, a car shot off in the opposite direction. Someone had followed me to the Dragon and waited in ambush. If Mehdi was in Germany, then who—?

In hopes of meeting Satan face-to-face I stomped the brakes, cut across the grass, harvested a shrub, and doubled back toward the intersection at an excessive speed.

The Devil made me do it.

I aimed for the taillights disappearing around the corner ahead. If he hadn't bolted, I might not have been able to identify the car. As it was, all I had to do was follow the yellow line up the middle of the street between honking commuters and an erratic UPS van that swerved into the parking lot of the Sof-Serve Ice Creme stand.

From under the seat I fished out my old red flannel shirt and unwrapped the pistol.

At the intersection cars were coming out of the Consolidated Insurance Company's barbed-topped security gate. Satan tapped his brakes for luck, then plunged through the red light, between cars. I wasn't so lucky, squeaking through a fracas of brakes and horns. Up ahead Satan leapfrogged down the line of traffic, drivers cringing over to the curb, making room as if for an ambulance. I followed his example.

It went on like this for half a mile. When he darted onto Route 9 for a stretch, past Lake Cochichituate and the old Black Label brewery, now a computer headquarters, I closed in to find I was chasing a coral-colored Chevy Citation with a CB whip antenna and a bumper sticker commanding: READ THE BOOK. His sporty felt hat shadowed his face.

Not Mehdi anyway, that was clear.

Store windows glowed in the dusk now. We flew past Scandinavian furniture, cheap suits, electronic organs, carpets, and The Bagel Man, then Satan suddenly hooked into a cutoff where the cross-traffic blocked him long enough for me nearly to catch him. Rather than shake my hand he bolted into the traffic, scampering out from under the wheels of a post-office trailer truck like a squirrel.

Passing the trailer truck down the road, I came face-to-face with a Natick cop coming the other way. He ducked over onto the curb. A few blocks later the Chevy surprised me by wheeling into a schoolyard, across a grassy playground and out the other side onto a dusky gray suburban street.

Dinky ranch houses lined the street, built on a dream after the War. They ended up in a new industrial park: offices of fortress concrete and dark-tinted glass; steel warehouses worthy of an army camp. In the distance the newest building was going up, its steel trusses like the brontosaurus skeleton in the Museum of Natural History.

He must have thought it would be like the playground, with an informal exit on the far side, because he squealed around the NO TRESPASSING signs onto the site, dodging the orange-striped traffic barrels and a crusty cement mixer, churning up a plume of dust. The other exit, the main one, turned out to have a wide security gate. Locked. In the thickening darkness, swerving into a U-turn, he flattened a sawhorse. He was getting flustered now, and as he was pulling out of the turn he skidded into a length of concrete sewer pipe. With a ripping noise the car rode up onto the pipe and came to rest.

By the time I pulled up he was out of the car and scrambling among the stacked pipe. I strapped on my Satan-tamer and got out. Nightfall was closing up the sky, though the horizon still glowed like light under the sides of a tent. As I expected, a bullet had punctured the rear door of the Volvo.

In this corner of the site they were putting in a water main, and he ran alongside the open trench. Just as I was beginning to think he'd ditched the pistol, he turned and pointed at me and bits of concrete exploded off a section of pipe ahead of me.

Rather than chance the security fence, he dropped into the trench. His felt hat bobbed along at ground level, then he ducked into the open tunnel of pipe. His footsteps clacked hollowly as he scurried into the depths. It looked as if the pipe would take him under the security fence. Maybe he'd panic in there. If he walked a mile into the ground and got spooked, then I could wait and he'd run out into my arms. Unless there were manholes open down the line and he was home free. I kicked my shoes off.

In Vietnam, the tunnels smelled like a greenhouse and swallowed you like a grave.

I kept low, scuttling in the trough of the pipe. This is hard on the lower back, as any chiropractor will tell you. In the dark I could hear his heels clopping. Behind me the opening was a faint gray disc hovering in the blackness.

He stopped to listen. His breathing was magnified in this giant speaking tube, a nervous sucking. I crouched down against the cool concrete. Water was dripping somewhere. When I looked back the opening had gone around a corner. The pipe wouldn't let me stand up, so I pitched forward onto my palms to straighten out my spine. Then he was moving again, more slowly now. I tucked my socks in my pocket and went after him in a running crouch, mouth open to silence my breathing, hardware in hand. I was prepared to fall on my face if he whirled about and fired. Whatever good that would do.

The pipe branched and I didn't realize it till I ran half up one wall and nearly knocked myself out. In the blackness ahead he said distinctly: "Oh shit."

I squeezed flat.

The detonation filled my head; the slug ricocheted crazily over me. I rolled into the other branch of the pipe for a moment and listened, the gunshot still singing in my ear. He fired again, a flat massive racket that drifted by me like smoke and left my heart rattling. We waited. A minute. Maybe more. The damp pressed against my skin, sweat leaked into my eyes. I couldn't believe how dark it was.

At last he stirred. Muttering, he began inching toward me. Once he passed I took a silent breath and pushed off, getting up speed, running pitched forward in the dark, one hand grabbing my other wrist, forearms out to protect my face.

He was closer than I thought.

When he heard me he wrenched about in time to catch my elbow under his chin. His pistol clunked against my ribs, and the pain, the flash of alarm, made me fall on him, elbows and knees, to disarm him. With a howl he collapsed and the pistol slid down the curved wall. The concrete skinned us both. I rolled him over and pinned his arm up behind him, and that was the match. Warmth pressed against my knee as his bladder let go. He was sighing like a colicky baby: "You can't do this to me."

To preserve his fingerprints I left his pistol where it was. Satan I hauled to his feet, pushing him up the pipe toward the world. He tried to shake me off.

"You're the one broke the law."

"Tell me about it."

"You broke into my house and my computer. You intimidated my wife. Impersonating a police officer, and—"

Then I placed the voice, the mix of defiance and self-pity. I could almost hear the snarl of those *Heritage Strike*

Force editorials. As for the pistol, I'd met it face-to-face once before in Frazier's backyard in Waltham. "I told you I was investigating a murder," I said, "and that was true."

"You acted like you were some kind of federal cop."

"You jumped to conclusions."

"It made my wife a nervous wreck. She thought I'd killed somebody."

"She's no fool. You hate a lot of people, Mr. Frazier."

"Well, you took the law into your own hands. Nobody should get away with that. That's invasion of privacy, it violates due process. It's communist tactics. I just gave you a taste of your own medicine."

"You put a bullet through my front door. Twice."

"I made my point."

"You could've killed my daughter, and you don't have any beef with her."

"A real army has to use live ammunition."

"Only this isn't a war."

Outside the evening air gave me a cool sweet smack in the face. A crooked moon and stars confused the darkness. The night glimmered on Donald Frazier's space-cadet wristwatch. It felt good to be back outside in space and time. He said, "Maybe I should've killed you when I had the chance."

Very close by someone said, "Hold it. Police."

"You're a witness," I said. A cop advanced on us. We found a private security guard and another Natick cop going over the Chevy and my Volvo with flashlights. The police had been chasing me since our brush with the trailer truck on Route 9. One of them, it turned out, had answered the call the night Donald Frazier had first shot up Meg's front door and I was able to refresh his memory.

"You had these threatening notes," he said, "from—what was it—something about the devil."

"The American Satan."

"That's right. And who's this?"

"Let me introduce you."

If you have enjoyed this book and would like to receive details of other Walker mystery titles, please write to:

> Mystery Editor
> Walker and Company
> 720 Fifth Avenue
> New York, NY 10019